Getting
Our Breath
Back

Getting Our Breath Back

SHAWNE JOHNSON

DUTTON

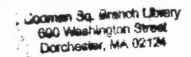
DUTTON **JUL** **2003**
Published by the Penguin Group
Penguin Putnam Inc., 375 Hudson Street, New York, New York 10014, U.S.A.
Penguin Books Ltd, 80 Strand, London WC2R 0RL, England
Penguin Books Australia Ltd, Ringwood, Victoria, Australia
Penguin Books Canada Ltd, 10 Alcorn Avenue, Toronto, Ontario,
  Canada M4V 3B2
Penguin Books (N.Z.) Ltd, 182–190 Wairau Road, Auckland 10, New Zealand

Penguin Books Ltd, Registered Offices: Harmondsworth, Middlesex, England

Published by Dutton, a member of Penguin Putnam Inc.

First printing, June 2002
10 9 8 7 6 5 4 3 2 1

 REGISTERED TRADEMARK—MARCA REGISTRADA

LIBRARY OF CONGRESS CATALOGING-IN-PUBLICATION DATA

Johnson, Shawne.
    Getting our breath back / Shawne Johnson.
        p. cm.
    ISBN 0-525-94654-3 (alk. paper)
        1. African American families—Fiction. 2. African American women—
Fiction. 3. Sisters—Fiction. I. Title.

PS3610.O38 G48 2002
813'.6—dc21

                                                        2002016094

Printed in the United States of America
Set in Goudy
Designed by Eve L. Kirch

PUBLISHER'S NOTE

For my husband, Dwayne,
and our daughters, Zola and Maya.
Where would I be, who would I be
without all of you?

Acknowledgments

I HAVE SO MANY people in my life who have made this novel possible.

My mother, La-verne Johnson, for loving and putting up with me. You always gave me the space, time, and encouragement to write.

My grandmother, Annie Johnson, for unwavering support, patience, and guidance.

My brother, Keith Johnson, for not allowing me to take myself too seriously.

My aunt, Cynthia Johnson, for always reminding me to have a good time.

My mother- and father-in-law, Sandra and Spencer Mercier, for always being supportive, loving, and kind. What would Zola, Maya, and I have done without both of you?

My in-laws, Donald Wharton, Dana Garnett, and Dionne Tyler, for the gift of their friendship.

The English Department at Bennett College, in particular Dr. Linda Beatrice Brown, Dr. Anne Mangum, and Dr. Audrey Ward for believing in my dreams.

The English Department at Temple University, in particular Dr. Sheldon Brivic and Dr. Lynda Hill for their patience and criticism.

My wonderful agent, Jimmy Vines, for sharing and respecting my vision and craft. Thank you, Jimmy, for baby pictures and baby gifts and treating me as a friend as well as a client.

My lovely editor, Laurie Chittenden, and everyone at Dutton for making the entire process of getting published exciting and fun. Laurie, your skill and kindness have been invaluable.

My sisters in spirit—Meg Strawbridge, Jamyla Bennu, Nadira Goldsmith, Nakia Scott, and Stephanie Henderson.

And at last, my beloved husband, Dwayne, and my babies Zola and Maya, for teaching me the true meaning of joy.

Getting
Our Breath
Back

Rose

ROSE WAS TIRED, skin-deep tired so that just a finger rubbing against the flesh of her lower arm or bare shoulder had her closing her eyes and leaning to the side, head light and easy and floating away. Mama sipping her tea and checking on her pie in the oven every ten minutes and trying not to listen to Violet ask Jerome where he been and when he coming back and why, and no answers. Nothing to hang a hope or a promise on, and Mama's eyes flinching each time Violet's voice weakened or faded out altogether.

Violet leaning against the kitchen counter, head in hands and phone cradled between shoulder and ear, dark skin washed pale and lean limbs pliant. "Jerome, I don't want to do this with you now. Let me go . . . No, no I don't understand . . . You know you not right . . ."

Violet struggling and holding in tears as Rose watched the flinching of Mama's eyes and heard Lilly slowly making her way to the kitchen and listened to the hesitation in Violet's voice and felt her heart, the red of her insides boiling,

1

heat radiating from her fingertips. Mama and sisters all tangled and bruised while upstairs in Rose's old bedroom her child, Imani, slept like there was nothing that she didn't need, nothing that she didn't have.

Late afternoon and Mama's kitchen filled with soft light and the kitchen floor spotless and shining and apple pie smelling like any second it was coming out the oven, and Rose wanted to go upstairs and get her child and go home.

Mama got up to pour herself another cup of tea. "Want some more, Rose?"

She ran her hands over the mess of her hair, soft and loose and reaching for the sky. "No, Mama. I'm okay. This peppermint tea?"

"I been mixing and dabbling. It's peppermint and just a little ginger."

Rose took another sip. "I can hardly taste the ginger."

Violet hung up the phone, dazed, and her face absolutely closed. Her dark slacks wrinkled and her cotton blouse clinging to skin damp with sweat and anxiety. She just made it to the table and Rose reached over to pull out her chair.

Violet tried to look up but her head dropped and rolled about on her shoulders. "We're going to talk when I get home."

Violet looking so fragile, the slenderness of her neck unable to support her head, the curve of her spine bowed from the weight of her body.

Violet showed her teeth, almost a smile but not quite because she looked like she could do real harm with those teeth if someone got too close. "I don't know. I just don't know."

Rose ran callused fingers over Violet's clenched fists. "You can't do nothing more than you doing, Violet."

Violet just stared at her, and Rose wanted to grab her and shake her hard because Violet always the meanest, always able to handle or take anything.

Mama went to get the apple pie out of the oven and Lilly came wandering in and everything and everyone stopped in mid-motion. Lilly, high yellow and so slim that she didn't look like a woman, resembled some underfed third-world brown child with huge eyes. Eyes shining from the high and feet always floating above the ground and locked hair hanging down the back and past the shoulders and long-sleeved shirt hiding the purple and red and blue bruises on her yellow skin. Her skirt moving around her body like some alive thing and Lilly looking almost dead except for the shining eyes and floating feet.

"Hey you all," she said and sat, unconcerned, and even the room was afraid to breathe, she looked that gone, and no one knew how to bring her back and all of them had tried. Rose was the first to exhale because Violet still wondering and worrying over Jerome and Mama wondering if this was really her child and Rose knew that it was Lilly. Lilly was best loved for a long time and she may be fucked up out of her head but her scent was still familiar, gardens in full bloom, and Rose knew that scent always, in absolute darkness or bullshit.

Lilly's forehead resting on the coolness of the kitchen table, her hair heavy and swinging all around her, and Rose reached out and placed her hands upon Lilly's head, feeling the warmth of the scalp through her locks. Hands moving over Lilly's hair and Lilly absolutely still and Mama finding the strength to bend down and take the apple pie out the oven and place it on the stove top to cool. Rose tried to think of Lilly like she was before she started staying out for days at a time, sucking in death through her body, stumbling home with arms tender and bruised.

Trying to find her sister in this woman that she really didn't know and whispering down to her to ask, "Baby, you doing all right?"

A long wait for the answer and during the wait Mama came back to the table and Violet's head stopped wobbling on her neck and Rose continued to stroke hair, separating heavy locks, gently twisting until the hair at the root coiled and then moving on to another lock. All of them waiting for Lilly to say something or not say something, just waiting.

Lilly turned her face toward Rose, cheek resting against the kitchen table and hair forming a veil across her mouth and nose and cheeks, only her eyes visible. "I'm fine, Rose of my heart. I'm fine." Eyes closing peacefully like sleep and face smooth like a child's and Rose and Mama and Violet all staring at her and staring at each other because there were no words.

Finally Violet said, "Lilly. Lilly, what the fuck—excuse my language, Mama—but what the fuck are you doing to yourself?" Rose hearing all of Violet's anger, anger at Jerome and herself and their life with two almost-grown sons falling away, all the time falling away because Jerome liked young girls, nibbled at necks still smelling of mother's milk, sucked at breasts that were mostly flat, spread thighs free of excess fat and smooth like stone.

Lilly stayed quiet, head still and eyes closed, and Rose wondered what she was thinking or feeling or if she had simply let herself go, letting go of the self and only the body remaining like Mama in church talking about what belongs to Earth and what belongs to Heaven and Rose all the time knowing that there was no relationship to spirit without the flesh. Lilly losing herself in flesh and needle sinking into skin and men who paid her to suck or fuck or feel.

Mama said, "Leave her alone, Violet."

Violet shook her head and the meanness that was all the time there beneath coy smiles and flirting eyes showed on her face. "Mama, we been leaving her alone all this time and look what's happened. I will not sit here and say that she is okay when she isn't. I can't do that because look at her. Look at her."

Rose shook Lilly lightly, no response, and she shook a little harder until Lilly lifted her head again. Thin face and huge eyes and wide mouth all familiar but the whole a person that she didn't quite recognize, and when and how did that familiar face become someone else even if the scent didn't change and what was she to do? Scent the same but everything else different. Body pounds lighter and tiny wrinkles from living too hard and losing too much weight around the mouth and skin no longer soft and warm but dry and cool to the touch. Lilly's face, stranger's face, looking blankly at her and she said, "Lilly, why don't you just go upstairs and sleep it off?"

Lilly pushing back her chair and rising to her feet and standing absolutely still and Rose and Violet and Mama trying to ignore bruises. Lilly floated through the kitchen and up the stairs and Mama asked, "Anyone want some pie?"

Rose shook her head. "No, I'm fine. I'm going to check on Imani and think about getting out of here, Mama."

She picked up Lilly's scent as soon as she hit the dining room, beyond the reach of kitchen and pie, gardens in full bloom, and Rose followed the trail of flowers through the dining and living rooms, up the stairs and to the door of Lilly's room. She hesitantly knocked and went inside and Lilly was lying on the hardwood floor directly in the sunlight coming in through the window, skirt around thighs and shirt lifted. Nothing but smooth leg and thigh and round breasts and Rose stared and wished that she had pencil and paper to sketch or that she was in her studio and Lilly like this burned in her mind to sculpt from wood and stone. Lilly always like some spirit woman, floating through the air and making of her own warm flesh ritual sacrifice. Rose closed the door and sat next to her on the floor, crossed her legs and pulled her wrap skirt around her knees so that their skin was touching. Imani slept hard and deep on Lilly's bed, curled into herself.

"I was hoping that you'd come up. That's the only reason I came through the kitchen really, to see you. Then all you staring at me and Mama looking like any minute she'd cry and Violet looking like she wanted to cuss me out and you looking like you wanted to pick me up and rock me and I couldn't think. Couldn't do anything else but put my head on the table and keep it there and not say a word."

"Okay. I'm up. What were you hoping on me for?" Rose

needing this time to be different, Lilly not miles and years away from her. Lilly's room the same room that they shared as girls, walls still covered in flowered wallpaper, floor still bare and hardwood gleaming, tops of dressers covered by baby dolls and stuffed animals. Little-girl room, nothing at all to hint at woman.

"Just hoping, that's all. Lay with me?"

Lying with Lilly in the sun, the wood of the floor cool against the exposed skin of leg and thigh, turning toward Lilly and curling into her, curling into the warmth despite the smell of some random man's sex and something dying slowly, skin falling from bone and bone bare and defenseless, and flowers, always flowers. Face protected between Lilly's head and the long, thick length of falling locks.

Watching Lilly drift into little-girl dreams. "I used to love sleeping with you. Remember? Skin to skin and safe," Lily said.

"Baby, what are you doing?"

"Rose, oh Rose. Taking names and keeping score . . . My whole body nothing more than a historical map or a historical past and nothing I can do but follow the roads already engraved beneath the skin."

Lilly's breasts in her line of vision, the smallness, and the pale yellow skin and the exposed childlike nipples. Wanting to grab a blanket and cover her and wash the stink of sweat off her skin and Lilly's love of words and playing with words and destroying words keeping her fragmented and swallowed by pen and paper, nothing worth saving, and paper filled with words and words and more words in the trash. "Lilly. Lilly, listen to me, poetry is killing you."

7

Lilly closing her eyes and long lashes resting against pale yellow skin, the skin about the forehead absolutely smooth and even. Rose watched Lilly's chest rise and fall and fall and rise slowly, almost holding her breath and letting it out in a great rush of words. "Not that, it's not that, and I know that you don't believe me and haven't even listened to me for some time. I know the kind of picture I present. In my head I hear all the time you all talking and wondering why I don't stop getting high, stop walking the streets, stop fucking up. I know what you all are thinking Rose, really. I think I must be telepathic or something. It's not poetry. It's not. I don't write anymore so it can't be, and if I don't write there's nothing to keep or constantly carry around and I carry enough with all this history beneath the skin without words always distorting my vision."

Rose trying to untangle and cut through and get to the heart of Lilly, hidden for so long behind nothing that made sense. "What are you talking about? Lilly, I have no idea of what you just said let alone what it meant."

Lilly turning away from her, smell of flowers and stale sex fading, and staring at the long length of back and the roundness of hip. "Where does that leave us?"

Staring at the length of her sister's back, the dark spots never quite faded from childhood chicken pox, the thin scar from a fall off the swings when they were both in elementary school. An entire life that included her written on the back of a sister that she didn't really know anymore. She kissed the exposed skin of Lilly's neck, finding warm flesh through cool hair, and left her there, sprawled out on the floor. Looking down on her and Lilly looked helpless, her body a light and insubstantial thing but she already had one child sleeping on the bed and she didn't know how to be a mother to one more, not one more.

"Lilly, I'm gone. Hear me, I'm gone."

Lilly not moving at all. "I hear you. Always."

Stepping over Lilly and making her way to the bed where Imani was still sleeping, still curled into herself. Rose picked up her child, Imani settling easy in her arms, an eight-year-old who was absolutely no weight at all.

Studio Time

EVERYTHING THAT ROSE NEEDED to know was in her hands, hands moving over smooth stone and lined wood, shaping women like women were all the time in Mama's house, like Mama and Violet and Lilly.

Daddy was sick for a long time, fading like bright old cotton sheets or all the colors of fall dulling and disappearing during winter. The last thing that Daddy did before he died was move them to North Thirty-third and West Allegheny Avenue in early 1957, when white people were scrambling to get out and middle-class black people moving in, looking for better schools and more opportunities and safer neighborhoods. North Thirty-third and West Allegheny Avenue was tree-lined blocks and green grass and driveways and front yards. The move sucked everything out of Daddy. His lung sickness was all the time with him, lung sickness eating at him while he sat around with a cigarette hanging from his mouth. By the time he died he was down to half a pack a day and couldn't get out of bed, lung sickness and not getting up the down payment for the house and helping take care of three girls and be a husband to Mama leaving him no air at all.

Rose, as a little girl, watched Daddy's chest heave and listened to the shallow sounds of Daddy's breath. Daddy was fighting for air like he was used to breathing something else and air was unknown. Eventually, all of Daddy's strength leaving him, his yellow skin pale and almost white, wrinkled and soft like something rotten. Daddy died and anything resembling male strength forever gone from the house and Rose holding on to Mama and Lilly and Violet's hands and all of them falling into each other the same way Daddy falling into the grave.

Rose wasn't hardly seven years old and for a long time it was hard to remember that Daddy was dead, for a long time she still looked and waited for him. They all slept with Daddy's old dress shirts and old slacks and old pillowcases, anything still holding something of Daddy.

Mama finally getting rid of all of Daddy's things, and the house was cleared of him entirely, just pictures, but the pictures were still and flat and had no scent. The scent of women slowly taking over the house like something good and sweet and easy to swallow. The scent seeping beneath Rose's skin, seeping into pores, directing her hands, and by the time Rose was ten years old Mama and Lilly and Violet were all she thought about drawing and, a little later, sculpting.

Rose coming home from school or coming in from out to play and Mama sitting at the table paying bills or writing in her journal or sewing someone something new and bright and warm. Mama's food was always on the stove and Lilly was always somewhere singing or holding meetings with her dolls and Violet was all the time on the phone or fixing her hair. An all-female household and an all-female support system and most of the time Rose felt safe and loved but sometimes she still hunted for Daddy's scent throughout the house, still looked for some kind of male something.

She left Mama's house almost grown and she was vulnerable away from Mama, all the time changing vital parts of her sense of self and her place in the world. A world where communities of women weren't acknowledged or cared about, just like entire communities of black folks terrorized down South and brutalized up North.

Lilly

EARLY FALL AND LEAVES UNDERFOOT, leaves golden and orange and red and fading dim green, and walking across the leaves, skipping like she used to when she was a little girl. Stopping and bending down and picking up a red-golden leaf and studying patterns beneath paper-thin skin the way she used to in first and second grade when the teacher sent them outside bundled and warm to look for leaves for their scrapbooks.

All those days were gone but the leaves coming back each year with early fall and leaves making music beneath her feet her favorite time of the year. Cool wind, not quite sharp with cold, against her face and in her hair, tugging at loose-fitting clothing, and the good smell of rot. Healthy smell of ashes to ashes and dirt to dirt not like trash day in any neighborhood anywhere in the city where things left out in trash bins on the sidewalk, the stench overpowering and bugs and birds and rodents gathering close.

Early fall as long as she can remember a time of beginnings and more important than rice and black-eyed peas and collards on New Year's Day and more important than dolls and notebooks and perfume on her birthday. Early fall and everything changing, changing and no death like the stillness of winter and no rebirth like the mess and rain of spring and no stagnant heat like the middle of summer. Early fall and change seamless and good and all the things that she really liked doing starting over for her, stomping through gold red orange leaves and wind against her face and sun like Mama or Daddy's hand resting against the crown of her head and marching to school with newly sharpened pencils and almost clean copy books.

Lilly walking through backstreets and side streets near North Broad Street and ever so often hearing the roar of the subway from underground, shaking the concrete beneath her feet and gold red orange leaves lifting and spinning over grated vents. Coming down off her high and everything just a little bit blurry and out of focus and she listened, listened hard to the music of the leaves beneath her feet.

Men and women fading in and out of her vision, bright fall jackets children wore dimming to black and white or shining so bright that she had to turn her head away and look at something else. There was a young girl holding her baby, no stroller or carrier, no baby bag even, just young girl and baby absolutely still and young girl absolutely sad. Lilly all the time looking into the faces of young girls, and so many of them had babies now, babies too small to even think about walking in their arms and sometimes bigger babies tugging at jackets and skirts and pants pockets. Young girls with child-smooth skin and vulnerable bitter mouths and they reminded her of the young girl she was before things went bad or she let things get bad and nothing that she could do but try to hold on.

Pale white Temple University students heading for the Southbound entrance on the subway and the train that would take them to the main campus and quiet, pristine classrooms and bored or kind and receptive professors. Temple University Main Campus and campus police at every corner, campus police keeping North Philly and Temple University totally separate so pale white kids could go to class and walk through campus and park their cars in front of people's homes. Older pale white Temple University medical students heading for the Northbound entrance on the subway and the train that would take them to Temple University Hospital and wiping away blood from knife cuts and putting in stitches and setting broken bones and no rest while on duty because North Philly was full of gang wars now. Boys and even grown men fighting over street corners or blocks, sometimes even just stoops, and everywhere anyone looked someone's dried blood dull red against cement pavements.

Lilly coming down off the high and tired and the music of leaves beneath her feet and watching people, places, things fade in and out too much. She sat down on the stoop of an abandoned house. Ten, even five years ago no abandoned houses really and now an abandoned house on almost every block and old people scared to leave their doors unlocked at any time of the day and especially not at night. Everything changing, changing so fast and no one with any time to catch their breath and where had all the rap that everyone was talking and spouting and screaming about ten and five years ago gone? All of it just gone like her days in first and second grade gathering red gold orange leaves for her scrapbook.

First time she stuck needle into flesh not too far from here, the stoop where she was sitting. She was a student at Temple University, her freshman year and she already knew that she wanted to be an English major, that she wanted to write about people, places, something, and writing the thing that she did best, the thing that she had been doing since learning to read and hold a pen. Temple almost ten years ago even more white than it was now and catching the bus and the subway from Mama's house to campus was like going blind into unknown territory even though the ride was no more than twenty minutes long. White faces and brilliant, clean classrooms and more white faces and food that tasted stale and old no matter where she bought it from on campus. All the vendors selling the same food, professors and students looking right through her so that she always felt that she was dripping, leaving valuable pieces of self and sense of time and place and what was really going on in her world like bird shit and empty cheese-steak wrappers on busy pavements.

Lilly sat on the abandoned stoop and thought about long-ago days and everything that she wanted to be and do and needles sinking into flesh and the face of the first boy she ever loved beaten and bloodied so that touching his skin was like touching the inside of an orange, squeezing orange pulp and all that blood and flesh oozing from between her fingers like something good and sticky and sweet. The next corner over from her abandoned stoop boys were singing, singing like the Temptations or the Dells and the wind picking up gold orange yellow leaves, picking up their voices and carrying it all to her. Voices that should be on the radio and the beat kept by the stomping of feet and the clapping of hands and the snapping of fingers. Singing groups like gangs spread all throughout the city, singing groups looking to make it big or liking the music, understanding the music and trying not to get caught up in knives slashing into soft skin and bats and pipes crashing down on hard bone.

Lilly thinking about the first boy that she loved and his face battered and blood dripping long before gang violence had everyone thinking black Mafia—as if the white Mafia weren't enough—and the only thing to worry and wonder and cry about was being stupid enough to wander into an all-white middle-class neighborhood anywhere in the city or coming face-to-face with a white police officer any time of the day, anywhere.

The singing from the other end of the street stopped and the boys walking away, heading to some other corner or maybe to someone's mama's house for something quick to eat and giving each other high fives and laughing loud enough for Lilly to hear and looking so young and new that she wanted to go with them.

Young and new like she was young and new ten years ago and summer ending and her freshman year at Temple University and walking lost around campus the first time that she saw him. He was easy to spot because there weren't that many brothers or sisters on the yard. Most of the black students lived at home, only crossed alien borders to attend class and check books out of the library. She was more than fifteen minutes late for a class because the subway was running behind schedule and considering not going at all when she saw him and a group of his friends handing out flyers that screamed Revolution Now! He was speaking to every black student who passed, grabbing at every black student and they were listening, forgetting about bullshit classes and almost done or almost researched papers. His voice sounding like North or West Philadelphia, the way brothers sounded talking to their mamas or sisters or girlfriends, that intimate and that smooth and that persuasive, and he was beautiful. Skin brown like Rose's and eyes almost black and long-lashed and mouth full and soft and long-limbed and lean, towering over everyone else.

Almost ten years later and hard for Lilly to see in her mind all that beauty sitting on cool cement stoop and coming down from the high and the horror of his face forever engraved behind the lids of her eyes and his body battered and limp like a little girl's stuffed anything used too long and thrown in the trash. Standing and watching and hearing him ten years ago and early fall come around again and cool wind against her face and she was clutching books and pens and loose papers against her chest and he smiled at her. Smiled at her and his smile like the way Daddy used to smile before it hurt him too much to do anything and she smiled back because Daddy's smile the same as safety and she knew that he wouldn't hurt her. Boys all the time doing all kinds of things to hurt feelings and ruin reputations and leave some girl all alone weeping and holding her heart and holding her womb in case heart and womb decided to fall, to jump out and run after a boy who wanted neither anymore.

Smile on his face and he came after her and the full force of his intimate West or North Philly voice directed straight at her and his hand resting lightly on her arm like he knew her, like they were old friends who hadn't seen each other in a while and he was sorry to have lost contact for so long.

His hand moving up and down her arm, over the fabric of her shirt, and she felt the heat of him through her clothes and he placed a flyer screaming Revolution Now! on top of the books and pens and scattered papers held against her torso like somebody's child and said, "This is for you. Been saving this one just for you. My name is Ben Carter and the revolution is now, sister. Now, and don't you let anyone tell you anything different, you hear me?"

His voice quiet and what he said just between the two of them and he was ignoring the crowd at his back and the professors and students walking past them and around them, giving them annoyed frowns that loudly suggested that they get the hell out of the way and do whatever it was they were doing somewhere else and not on university property and not on university time. She simply fell into him, fell into him like falling into Daddy's arms when he was still strong enough to catch her and Ben Carter stood still for her and willingly and gladly accepted all of her weight. She said, "My name is Lilly."

Giving him her name and everything that she was in her wide smile and falling like invisible streaks of tears or wrinkles of laughter at the corners of eyes and braced around the mouth.

His hand stayed on some part of her for almost the entire year, his breath her breath and his body her body, and touching him, loving him was almost like loving herself—that easy and that seamless. Touching and bodies clenched tight together in pleasure or holding each other tenderly and Revolution Now! and Huey P. Newton and Black Power and they were kings and queens and his twin bed in the dorm room all and every bit of blackness that they needed or wanted. She kept studying even when she realized that there really was no point in anything that she learned and she had to be suspicious of textbooks and academic articles and professors and all the agendas floating out there just waiting for anyone who looked like her and talked like her and came from where she came from to stumble in and around.

She was happy and Mama was happy for her and Rose and Violet and she felt like she was finding her place in the world, finding her place and she had been adrift for so long. Adrift ever since Daddy died and she was his favorite girl and then he was gone and she was left to dig for the scent of him in his chair and old blankets and his clothes before Mama finally got up the nerve to throw them all away. Then there was nothing left at all but pictures of Daddy, Daddy smiling at some holiday, Daddy standing with all of his girls in front of the house, Daddy laughing and his smile wide and his mouth open. Most of the pictures of Daddy ended up in her room, hanging from her walls, stuck under the corners and edges of mirrors, and everywhere she looked

Daddy staring back at her and it still wasn't enough, the pictures just hinting at the person that Daddy was and leaving her always wanting his hands on her hair and his lips on her forehead and his breath, smelling like cigarettes and rum, against any part of her face.

Ben her first real boyfriend and she didn't know enough to ask questions, didn't know enough to wonder over who he was and where he was and what he was doing when he was away from her. Eighteen years old and she just assumed that all his time not spent talking to her or listening to her or touching her spent on Revolution Now! and Black Power. Ben and all the other brothers on campus always talking about and for black people and all that talking making male voices hoarse and eyes bloodshot from trying to keep up with classes and papers and exams and Revolution Now! and Black Power, most of the men all the time tired and all the time angry and trying not to falter. Trying not to get caught up in good grades and good jobs and keeping quiet to avoid consequences like being kicked out of school or constantly harassed by campus police and city police and the weight of it all.

Sometimes Lilly went to Ben's dorm room in the middle of the day, middle of the day and the campus loud and gasping with folks and inside his room everything quiet and dark because the shades were drawn. She took off her clothes for him, didn't think about missing classes or finishing papers or all of the things that she had to do. Her body and breath and touch a willing dumping ground for all his shit.

The first time he tied belt around her arm and stuck needle into her flesh she wasn't scared or even surprised. She loved him and he had found something to make the whole thing easier and loving him was getting hard, loving him no longer colored by little-girl fantasies of princes and princesses, of ever after and always. All the time trying to take care of her needs and his needs and Revolution Now! and Black Power and she wanted something to make the whole thing easier just as much as he did. Easier when every black male somebody on campus thought, before they found out that she was Ben's woman, that she was available to suck or fuck or hurt. Easier when Ben ignored her or talked down to her because she was a woman and her position in Revolution Now! and Black Power was marginal at best, her ideas not as good and her anger nothing but hysterics because she had breasts and ass and uterus.

The first time Ben sunk needle into bulging flesh and vein the feeling almost like orgasm, her whole body welcoming the breaking down, the tearing down of all of its most vital parts. Her whole body becoming zombielike and a lightness in her chest, just above her heart, her arms and legs all the way gone and she was a drifting and floating thing, drifting and floating high above the ground, angel child. The high so sweet that they got high whenever they could afford it, whenever Ben hunted down white boys on campus selling on the side, putting themselves through school, and wore long-sleeved shirts to hide the bruises. Lilly didn't mind the bruises on her arms, didn't mind it at all, especially when she was floating, drifting, because then bruises looked like art, like intricate patterns and paintbrush strokes and she thought her arms a masterpiece and wished that everyone could see and admire.

It wasn't Revolution Now! or Black Power that changed their lives forever, made them different people and who they were scraped completely away like peeling back layers and layers of paint. It was North Philly outside of the reach and range of Temple campus police and Philly city police, North Philly where police didn't care what happened as long as it didn't spill into Temple or parts of the city where upright citizens swept their steps and small squares of pavements in front of their houses and kept their lawns and yards well tended. It was North Philly and Ben Carter sprawled out on dirty cement, the bottom half of his body hanging loose and broken from the curb onto the tar and filth of the street. Ben Carter with face bloodied and unrecognizable, flesh soft like something going bad in open air, and arms, legs, feet, hands at impossible angles like he was the main attraction at the circus and all kinds of people willing to pay to see what all he could do.

No one knew what happened. Ben trying to talk through a mouth full of blood and cracked and broken teeth and rushing to see him at the hospital and he was choking on his own blood and all the doctors and his mama kept telling her that he was going to be okay and the doctors kept poking and prodding at the bruised and raised skin of his arms. Doctors looking at her as if they could see needle stuck in her arm and drug moving through her body.

Studio Time

THE STUDIO ALMOST COLD, windows open to let in chilling fall breeze and fall breeze raising goose bumps and hair on her bare arms and every now and then she pulled herself away from her worktable to rub dirty, dusty hands against cool flesh. Rose thought that maybe she should close the windows, but the good smell of fall coming in with the cold and closing the windows like admitting defeat.

Sketching two little girls playing a hand game, hands moving fast and eyes and mouths laughing. Two little girls sitting on the ground cross-legged with skirts raised to the knees and panties showing and pigtails bouncing each time they slapped hands. She was trying to remember the songs, the songs she and Lilly used to sing hands clapping against each other and hands always trying to move faster and faster and faster until palms turned bright red and stung from the heat. They played hand games almost until they were grown, played hand games and talked to dolls and kept diaries and told each other secrets like secrets between them once spoken aloud were forever shut and sealed away.

Lilly for all that time after Daddy died almost hers entirely. Rose had to share Lilly with her books and writings but she didn't even mind that because Lilly was always telling her stories and reading to her from her journal and Lilly's writings were almost her writings, they were that close. Tied up in one another and Violet somewhere in the background, frightening and preoccupied with boys and men. Violet had time for them only when she felt like it, when she was lonely and needed a warm body to sit in her lap and hold or when she was angry and stubborn and stomping about the house looking for someone to yell at, make cry.

Wasn't until Lilly started college that Rose felt the first pulling away, a break in the seam of their relationship, and the break was like watching Daddy put in the ground all over again and Mama walking around for days, weeks, years blindly and her insides hanging from her, trailing behind her like tears. Lilly grown and no more time for hand games and no more time to tell her stories or lie with her in the middle of the night or long, lazy afternoons, just the two of them quiet and sometimes sleeping and sometimes watching the patterns that light made across the floors and walls and ceilings.

Lilly bringing home that boy who died later on and Lilly getting high with that boy, although no one knew it then. All of them just puzzled and watching the gift, the magic that was always Lilly's flicker and fade and dim like a candle or fire getting too little air. Rose all the time missing Lilly and going places where she should not have been. Running the streets with girlfriends and all her girlfriends almost the same, sweetly brittle, young and brash, sugary mean about the mouth, unraveling at the edges. Her girlfriends a poor substitute for Lilly but hanging out with them was better than sitting at home and waiting for Lilly to stop by for her, dropping in and out like Rose was just some stranger woman that she knew in passing.

Lilly for a long time after Daddy's death the one thing that Rose held on to. Lilly all the sudden gone and nothing to hold on to and reaching for whatever fit easily and comfortably in her hands and heart, not realizing that easy is paid for later on.

Rose

MID-MORNING AND ROSE COMING BACK from the grocery store, arms laden with bags of food. She spotted Lilly singing in the streets, just singing like she was Aretha and had a voice like gold, like she was on stage at the Apollo in front of a thousand screaming people, and asked, "What the hell do you think you're doing and when is this shit going to stop?"

Lilly just stood there, the sun shining behind her, shining right through her so that she looked like some drugged-up mystical fallen angel, talking through wide pretty lips that were cracked, twirling about in a yellow dress that was beautiful and soiled. "What am I doing, sister dear, the Rose of my heart? Oh, baby, I'm on the lookout. I'm on the hunt. 'Cause see, I can smell it. I'm going to find it and let it take me anywhere it wants to go. Maybe to Senegal, that's where we went last time, and I spent the night in the arms of a prince, can you see? Me with an honest-to-God fucking prince! Ain't no way that shit going to happen when I'm mired in the filth of North Philadelphia.

"And I love my people, you know I do. I can quote Malcolm and Martin and Fannon and Baldwin for days for weeks for years but all this blood and mayhem just fucks with me, really fucks with me. So I hunt, I find, I go. Maybe I'll bust Mandela out of jail and kill all the crackers who fuck up shit over there just like they fuck up shit over here."

Rose watched her as she swayed and moved like she was her own personal dance troupe, like she was onstage and not on a sidewalk lined with bottles and cigarette butts. "Oh, Lilly, baby, this shit has to stop. What am I going to do? Waiting for you to turn up dead or raped by these no-good bastards masquerading like they men, giving you this shit that's no good for you so that they can grab a fuck. And you, like some old crazy Civil Rights leader gone astray— and we in the fucking seventies, fucking 1976, it ain't the sixties anymore. You went to Senegal, you going to South Africa to bust Mandela out? Well, first you got to be clean, do you hear me? When you high you don't go nowhere, you don't become anything. You just high and fucked up and you are hurting me, you hurting me so bad because we, you and I, we always loved each other best. Come home with me. Come home with me."

Lilly kissed her, smelling sweet and fresh like she wasn't a drug addict at all, but wandering through lush fragrant gardens and not the brick and concrete of the city. "Darling Rose, go home. Kiss Imani for me. I'll see you soon. When I come back or down or get a grip. No longer mad or crazy or high. And maybe we can sleep in the same bed like we used to do when we were little, see? And I'll hold you close, 'cause I always loved you best, too." She was crying, a ghost of a woman, still familiar, still beautiful but the beauty was fading like she was fading and Rose hugged her and let her go.

Walking home to her house, walking through the neighborhood and so much changed from when she was a little girl. Young boys on the corner, talking loud and faces shiny and wet with arrogance and confidence and fear. Young girls sitting on their steps with hair and nails done and flirting mouths and eyes not quite grown but too hard to be called innocent. Trees still hanging over streets and neighborhood still green, anywhere in North Philly just a minute from the park. The people different, people tired and no waiting for better days and better times.

Rose went home to her house and she burnt incense and lighted candles and ran a bath, trying to get the scent of flower gardens, the scent of Lilly, off of her. The bath was hot and she added peppermint oil and sank into it until only her hair and eyes were visible above the water.

Coming out of the tub was like coming out of the womb, a safe, warm, wet space. Rose wanted to stay there as long as possible but there were half finished stone and wood women calling to her, yelling and shouting at her. Her art was a celebration, a dance, a rhythm that she lost herself in. The women, her women, but not really, like Imani was her child, but not really. The women, like Imani, had their own personalities, their own laughter and smiles and tears and secrets. It was the mystery of it all that kept Rose in her studio on the second floor of the house. Mystery in shaping a body that was so like hers, but not hers, mystery in watching the blood from her cuts dripping down upon wooden women open and willing and ready to receive life.

She had her first showing at twenty-three, and she was so nervous, so terrified because beneath the stone, beneath the wood and secrets and smiles and cries of all the women was one woman—herself. She was fighting for her life then, working two jobs, sculpting in the evenings, taking care of a five-year-old girl child because it all had to mean something—who she was, her child, her art. She had watched as people who knew nothing about her wandered among the women, touched and fondled and oohed and ahhed and it was almost a form of rape. But she stayed, and talked, and kept a grin on her face because this was it, the whole thing meant the difference between struggling, struggling forever or taking a deep breath and living. All the women in the show sold, and that was another kind of sadness, another sorrow. She missed them.

Rose dried herself, and smoothed lavender oil on her skin. She pulled on jeans and a camisole, studied her hands. She didn't mind the fact that she didn't have pretty hands, although her hands had been lovely at one point, skin soft and tender and nails perfectly shaped and trimmed. That was before she fell in love with stone and wood and women. She tried to recall which came first, the love of women or the love of stone and wood. Perhaps women; she lived in a house full of women smells and women ways and women talk. She shared a room with Lilly and watched, because Lilly was two years older, as her body rounded and softened and she was amazed at it all, amazed that the sister she loved best, better than anyone, had this whole other person living inside of her. Rose, as a girl child, waited for her own metamorphosis, for the woman hiding inside of her to come out and make herself known.

Mama thought she was crazy when she began bringing limbs of wood home to work on in the basement. Mama didn't understand that the wood was living, breathing, that it told her secrets and allowed her to shape it only with its permission. She started with women because the wood didn't mind being shaped into a woman's body, being anointed with a woman's soul. In Mama's house women were all that she knew, everything that she loved, all that she looked forward to being. Mama working all the time to put food on the table, and Violet baby-sitting when she was a teenager and hot in the pants with better things to do than sit at home with two little sisters. And Lilly gliding and floating on the air, reciting poetry, and humming gospel like she really was some spirit creature, not made for the real world at all.

The telephone rang, Rose picked up, and it was Violet furious and raging. "He's cheating on me, cheating on me, Rose. Rose, I want to kill him, I swear I want to kill him."

Rose sat down on her bedroom floor and crossed her legs; she could hear Violet panting and imagined her dark brown face and hands clenched and throbbing, saw her standing and looking like she had in Mama's kitchen—dark skin pale and long limbs fragile. "Violet, Violet are you sure? You absolutely positive?"

Violet so angry she was heaving, the words just tumbling out. "Of course, I'm sure. Been more than sure for a while, you know that. He didn't come home all night. All night, Rose. He's never done anything like that before, well maybe once or twice, but he always apologized. And when I asked him about it he just stared at me like I wasn't making any sense, like I was speaking some foreign language and he just walked away. Just walked away."

"I'm so sorry. I'm so sorry."

"I don't know what to do, I don't. All these years of cooking and cleaning, taking care of two boys. What else was I supposed to do? What more could I have done?"

"You want me to come over and sit with you? You want to come over here?"

"I don't know. Imani home from school yet?"

"Not yet, in a little bit."

"I don't want to come over ranting and raving and scaring that child."

Rose laughed, and Violet also, even though her laughter was strained. "Come over. I'll feed Imani, sit her down to do homework and then out to play. You and I can talk. I'll fix you some tea . . ." And she was thinking, *Why do you put up with this mess, Violet? This is not the first night spent alone, not the first tears and raging, not the first pain. Why stay? Sister who held my hand when no one else would or could, sister who helped me bring my child into the world.*

"What? No coffee?"

"See, that's part of the reason why you stressed now."

Violet let loose with a loud snort. "No, baby. I think I'm stressed 'cause my husband's out fucking some young girl or maybe a whole bunch of young girls and I can't do anything about it. I can't even think right now."

"Come over."

"Maybe."

"I love you."

"Me, too. 'Bye."

The line went dead and Rose just sat there, the red walls of her bedroom surrounding her, enclosing her in warmth and light and incense burning. The first time Mama saw her bedroom she exclaimed, "Why, Rose, this looks like a whorehouse!" She was horrified and Rose had to laugh. Mama had no color in her house, nothing but a lot of white walls and light because Mama refused to live in a dark and shadowed house. Rose needed color, color on the walls, color on the sofas and chairs and rugs. Her bedroom, her house was the center of her existence, space that circulated and pumped and beat with a life all of its own, renewing her, cradling her like the child she cradled in her stomach for nine months.

She held conversations with Imani while the baby rested and developed inside of her. Rose wanted a girl child because she thought that maybe she would have to do it all alone and a girl child seemed easier—a daughter, a sister, a friend. She lay in bed at night in Mama's house late in pregnancy terrified at the thought of childbirth but anxious to see her child. Imani came and birth was painful and excruciating and lasted eighteen hours but it was worth it because afterward Rose held this crying, red-faced child in her arms, so like her but not like her at all: Imani.

Rose heard Imani's key in the lock, lifted herself from the floor and went down the steps to greet her child. Imani was flushed and laughing, always laughing and dancing in circles and so happy with herself that Rose smiled. "Hey, little girl, what got in you today?"

"Mommy, I got an A on my spelling test and I'm so glad because we studied and studied and I thought that maybe I missed a word but I didn't . . . I got them all right, all of them, Mommy." Imani was twirling and hopping about, her braids flying around her head.

"Yay, Imani! Come give me a hug." And Imani rushed into her arms, warm body smelling like outdoors and milk and crayons and paper—all the things that make up an eight-year-old girl. Rose held her tight because she was so fine and so precious—the most valuable thing that she had.

Imani yelped, "Mommy, let me go."

Rose released her and they settled comfortably together on the stairs, Imani cuddled in Rose's lap.

"What we having for dinner?" Imani asked, tugging gently at the tails of Rose's braids, a habit she'd had since she was a baby.

Rose shrugged and began to rock slowly, knowing that times like these were coming to an end, that Imani, in a few years, wouldn't want to sit in her lap and be rocked. "I haven't given it much thought. Since you got the A and all, what do you want?"

"Anything?"

"Yeah, within limits. No brownies or sundaes or chocolate bars."

"Okay. I want tacos and corn chips and salsa."

"All that, huh?"

"Yup. And I'm going to eat it all, too."

"I'm scared of you. Why don't you go put your things away and get cleaned up?"

"Now?" Imani asked, reluctant to leave.

"In a little while, then. I'll hold you as long as you let me."

They sat there, the hardwood stairs cool beneath them, and outside they could hear children playing and grown folk laughing. Imani had left the door open and a nice breeze came in through the screen door, smelling like fall and winter close on its heels. They had lived in the house, on the small block, in the neighborhood full of people who looked like them and talked like them, for a little over two years. They moved out of Mama's house after Rose had her first showing and everything sold and there was money to spare. Not that they were rich, the fear of poverty, of not having enough to feed and clothe and house herself and her child was always there in the back of Rose's mind. They were doing well, her women were selling, and she had a nice following, people whom she could count on to buy a piece, and she wasn't quite twenty-seven, that was a good start. But things could change, and it was the thought of change that kept her awake at night. She didn't want to leave North Philly. This was home, where she was born and raised and nurtured and loved. She left North Philly once, with Imani's father. When she was open and new, like a child, but with a woman's smile and shape.

She, Rose, sister of Lilly and Violet, was inherently brilliant, inherently beautiful, inherently black. So she left North Philly with this man who was twenty-three and so different from her, from everyone that she knew that he almost seemed alien. His name was Charles and he was a writer and he wrote everything down—what he saw, how he felt, what he thought she should feel. Words on paper overwhelmed Rose. It was pristine and neat and somehow horrifying; words on paper didn't mean anything or maybe they meant everything.

Charles lived and breathed words like Lilly and the words why she thought she loved him. Rose lived and breathed women and wood and stone. And how wonderful it was at first to have someone interpret the world of words for her, Lilly getting high and making no sense at all. How lovely to ask Charles, what does this mean and why is this there on this particular piece of paper just so and get an answer that made sense, that made words accessible and not a puzzle to labor and cry over.

The summer of her eighteenth year, living on South Street with a man who was familiar, because loved, and unfamiliar because different, not of the same understanding, she was happy. Happy even though it was the tail end of the sixties and everyone was dying or dead, Martin and Malcolm, and Lumumba. Or everyone was leaving, ex-patriots off to Africa even though poor and black because there was always money to travel, to go, and who wanted to be a part of a country that was so sick in any case? She and Charles created a New World, a world of birth and forgiveness. They were going to rewrite history and bring everyone who was dead or dying or simply left out back into the fold. In the third-floor apartment that they shared there was always burning incense and green plants and sacred waters. She painted the walls dazzling shades of royal blue and ruby red and emerald green. Jewel tones that made the apartment, which wasn't very nice or big or bright, seem huge and light and filled with air. They had no furniture, a mattress for a bed and cushions to sit on. The floors were covered with African and Indian prints. James Baldwin and Jimi Hendrix gazed imperiously from walls.

Their lovemaking was a prayer. Charles wasn't the first, but in the beginning his touch was profound, could move her, perhaps not physically, but emotionally so that she was vulnerable and still beneath the weight of his hand, the long length of his body. On the mattress on the floor their bodies moved together and sighed together and laughed together. Weekends they would lie in bed like spoons holding each other and listening to people pass if it were nice out, and listening to stillness, sometimes rain, if the day were gray and overcast. They worked when they had to for money, but art was their life, they were innocent, childlike, thinking that they could make the world whatever they wanted it to be.

When the dream cleared she was alone and pregnant and back in North Philly and Charles was gone. Sometimes she wondered if he had ever really been, if he were simply words on paper that could mean nothing or anything or everything. Imani the result of Immaculate Conception and she a Saint.

Studio Time

S HE LIKED TO WORK with deep, dark wood best. Wood smooth and supple and alive beneath her hands like skin but so different because of the hardness and coolness. There was no warmth beneath the dark flesh of wood, nothing to hint at pumping blood and beating heart.

Sculpting was for her like telling a story, a story like Violet's pain or Lilly insisting that her yellow flesh was nothing more than ritual offering.

Her own story the hardest to tell because there was no beginning or middle or end, just this long, continuous line of shit happening to her and it was hard for her to make any kind of sense out of her own shit.

Huge moments like meeting Imani's father when she was seventeen years old. Seventeen years old and hair in long braids down her back because she never saw any need to perm her hair even before Black Power and natural this and natural that because she simply liked the feel of her hair. Liked to braid it or comb it out and wash it and feel its softness and curliness and thick and lush nappiness. Seventeen years old and she really didn't understand that her hair wasn't the only thing that was lush, that her body was over-ripe and men were all the time looking and watching and waiting for her to fall, fall from the tree of Mama's influence and lose the last vestiges of little-girl smiles and little-girl pleasures.

She was innocent still even though she had let a boy before Charles come into her, a boy, Wayne, she loved with flesh warm and solid and a penis long and rigid sliding in and out of her and holding her still with arms and orgasms and sweetness. The Vietnam War took Wayne away and then he was blown from the face of the earth like a shooting star without any sense of direction, moving away instead of toward solid ground. She wasn't untouched but the innocence was still there and it added to her lushness so that men were all the time wondering about her and she wasn't oblivious just heartbroken and uninterested, recovering from first love and loss and the terror of really growing up and not just playing at it like little girls sometimes do, like little girls sometimes spend all of their childhood playing dress-up and makeup and house and mommy.

Seventeen years old and all of a sudden playtime was over and a woman's sadness beginning to form small creases and lines at the corners of her eyes. Wrinkles in child-smooth skin and sitting at a table in a bar with one of her more adventurous girlfriends on South Street and watching men sit down next to them and talking to them and sending them on their way. The bar filled with all kinds of people—black, yellow, brown, red, white—and the tension that held tall those different kind of people over race and Martin and Malcolm and Civil Rights not quite as heavy or as thick. Summer of 1966 and most people in Philly just and simply tired and looking for places to rest and someone kind and soft and not made hard by evening news and freedom rides and the March on Washington and Vietnam and constant screaming from the South and cities going up in flames all across the North.

Her girlfriend, Cookie, brown and round and all smiles and brittle sweetness and something like challenge coating her breath so that the men moved close to her and wanted nothing more than to breathe her in. Rose paled beside all that brashness and strident sweetness, paled even though she was wearing her favorite red skirt (borrowed from Lilly) and white blouse and her hair fantastic on her head and her mouth painted a deep red, lips shining wet.

Cookie held court, and Rose didn't mind because she was still heartbroken after all, and these were men. Men with girlfriends and wives and cars and houses or apartments of their own and she really didn't know what she was supposed to do with them or what they wanted to do with her. The bartender fed them too-sweet drinks and she and Cookie sat at the bar with legs crossed and Cookie was talking to some man, dark-skinned and big and breath smelling like pipe smoke and gray at his temples and his hand was lingering casually on her thigh. Big hand with rings and a watch at the wrist and fingernails wearing clear polish just sitting and rubbing against the deep brown of Cookie's flesh through her short skirt and Cookie was sipping her drink and giggling. Cookie looking twenty-five or thirty years old and not like she just turned seventeen and still shared a room with her younger sister in her mama's house and had to be home on the weekend before eleven o'clock at night.

Rose sat watching the hand on Cookie's thigh, the hand always moving and sometimes moving high and sometimes low and Cookie not paying Rose the least bit of attention. Cookie sipping at her drink and cutting her eyes like she really knew what she was doing and this wasn't some huge game that she was practicing for a later engagement and saying, "And why should I do that? I don't know you that well. I only do that with friends."

Rose wasn't sure what the *that* of the conversation was but she listened hard as the man said, "Darling child, don't you know I want to be your friend? That's all I'm thinking about at this moment. Being your very good friend."

Cookie running her hands through her permed hair and smiling and showing all teeth. "But I have enough friends. Really. I don't think that I can stand just one more."

The man moved his hand higher up Cookie's leg, almost under her skirt, and Cookie's smile wavered with shock and pleasure and the man said, "I'm going to buy you another drink. That's what I'm going to do."

"My friend, too?" Cookie asked.

"Yeah, if she wants one. Do you want one, sweetheart?"

Rose shook her head. "No, I'm fine." She was thinking that it was Friday night and ten o'clock and that meant that they only had an hour to get back to Cookie's mama's house in North Philly without all hell breaking loose and walloping their asses. Cookie didn't look like she was going anywhere anytime soon, not while that man's hand was making her feel all sorts of things and his hand was under her skirt now and Rose was embarrassed to be staring at something that intimate and she looked away. Sitting on the other side of her were a group of men closer to her own age and one man, the man that was sitting the farthest away from her, was staring so hard that she felt him sucking her in, sucking her in and she had never been looked at that hard before, like he could see beneath the skin and was fascinated by her muscle and bone and beating blood.

His friends talking to him and he just kept staring and she could hear Cookie say, "No, don't do that." Cookie sounding uncertain and the pleasure there just beneath the voice so that all ears were tuned toward her and Rose was being swallowed by some stranger's eyes.

The man with his hand on Cookie's thigh, beneath her skirt, saying, "Okay. Okay, baby. I won't do that. I won't."

Rose knew that Cookie knew that whatever he was not going to do he was going to try again and it was quarter after ten and really time to go. She smiled at the man staring at her because she was polite and Mama raised her to acknowledge anyone staring dead straight at her and he smiled back and he had a nice smile and she was thinking that that wasn't hard or complicated at all when he hopped down off his bar stool and walked past his friends to her. He was long of limb and tall and thin and his features were fine, eyes like early morning and mouth wide. Cookie was absolutely quiet next to her and breathing hard and she wondered just where the man's hand was under Cookie's skirt and this other man was leaning in toward her, smiling and saying, "You are the most beautiful thing I've ever seen and I know

42

that sounds trite and unoriginal but looking at you I can't form an original thought, not one. I know that I was staring at you like, I don't know, like I had never seen a woman before and I was going to lose my mind and at any moment start dribbling. I'm sorry for that. Really. And then you smiled at me and I thought that it was okay and appropriate for me to come over and say something to you before you left and we never crossed paths again. So. Okay. My name is Charles and I would like to see you again if you don't think I'm too crazy."

Rose was absolutely stunned and next to her Cookie was incoherent and trying hard not to make any noises and her legs spread wide beneath the bar. He was the last man she ever saw herself wanting and his skin was paper-thin. "Hi, Charles. I'm Rose. We were just leaving, really. But it was nice meeting you and maybe I'll see you later . . ."

"Tomorrow? For lunch or dinner, whatever?"

Cookie was absolutely limp beside her and she was feeling dangerous and grown and fearless and she let it all go to hell. "Okay. I'm staying with my friend for the weekend. I'll give you her number and you can call me there if you like."

That was how she met Charles, while Cookie got finger-fucked at a bar. They just barely made it back to Cookie's mama's house before eleven. She was moving toward something new and leaving something behind and Cookie shining bright with pleasure.

Rose

ROSE ON HANDS AND KNEES waxing hardwood floors, old rag in her hands smelling like Mama's house because Mama's hardwood floors were always clean and polished so clear like reflections of faces off of clean, calm waters. Starting in the dining room and working her way out because once she got to the front door she could go sit on the steps in front of the house with sketch pad and pencil and play and try to get a feel for the woman or women inside of her, different and the same, trying to get out. Imani in school and the house quiet and how nice it was to be an artist who actually made enough money to live so that she could wax floors in the middle of the week instead of working and only have time for cleaning and child and dances and dates and life during the weekends.

Rhythm to cleaning the floors like dancing, hips rolling back and forth and shoulders moving from side to side and her reflection—hair wild on head and face young with sweat—looking up at her and she remembered being eighteen and just pregnant and unwed and terrified and living with Charles. Dancing with Charles, bodies close together and trying to find the rhythm, Imani growing strong between them. Charles was long-limbed and tall and lean and she was round and soft and small. Their bodies moved differently, always pulling against and away from each other. When they danced most of the song was spent trying to figure out where arms and legs and hands and feet went—it wasn't effortless—and she supposed that if she hadn't been eighteen and pregnant and wanting him because he seemed like the thing to want she would have been suspicious of the way their bodies moved together—bodies that were never meant to know each other intimately, only in passing.

Charles was only the second man to really touch her and when they danced or any time that his hands were on her she was still, still and quiet facing the enormity of him, the enormity of eyes like morning and what they could possibly be to each other and words all the time falling from his mouth like Lilly. Words written or typed on paper and paper scattered haphazardly about their small apartment like Mama had knickknacks all throughout her house.

In the beginning, before eighteen and pregnant and living together and fighting and hating each other on South Street, Rose thought that they were going to make it. Make it even though South Street was not at all like the place where she came from, Mama's house in North Philly. Mama's house not too far from Fairmount Park and faces that looked like her and people who talked like her, still a hint of the South in their voices. South Street different and everyone had a cause or a protest and everyone all the time arguing over big points or small points and some faces that looked like her and more faces that didn't and almost everyone waiting for the blow to fall.

The night she met him was almost unreal for her because she and Cookie were both a little drunk and it was just hard to imagine that the entire thing took place. It made no sense at all because when they woke up the next day they were children sleeping together in Cookie's bed. Cookie's mama and daddy were at church and they were eating a breakfast of too-sweet cereal, child's face on the box, when the phone on the kitchen wall rang and Cookie jumped up to get it in her short white nightgown that just covered her ass. Rose paid absolutely no attention, kept eating her cereal, only looked up from her bowl when Cookie said, "Rose, it's for you."

"I know that's not Mama calling for me this early."

Cookie just shook her head, eyes wide. "Uh-uh, it's not your mama, Rose."

Rose heard Charles' voice and the night before hidden beneath waking up in a white-walled bedroom in a single bed with her best friend and dolls staring and wearing little-girl nightgowns came rushing back and she was almost grown again.

Charles on the phone overwhelming her with words. "Hello. I hope it's not too early or too late or too whatever because I was just thinking about you. All the time since last night thinking about you and how soft and strong your hair looked, how brown your skin was, how lovely your mouth was. All the time thinking about you and I wanted to see you again, today if I can. Is that good for you?"

Rose leaning against the wall, sharing the phone with Cookie and both of them pushed by his words into silence. Rose thinking about Lilly and the way that she thought that there was no one in the world that could possibly say things the way that Lilly said them, like words were a natural extension of the body like legs, arms, hands, and feet. Cookie's eyes were huge in her head and she mouthed, "Say something, girl."

Rose stared at the kitchen table, at her bowl. The milk was turning pink from all the food coloring and sugar and the cereal was getting soggy. Next to her bowl stood the cereal box, child's face on the front looking at her. Child's hair blond and eyes a light, light brown, and skin pale and smile wide and teeth white. She didn't know where to even try to begin. Cookie shoved her, hissed, "Say something."

"Rose?" Charles asked.

She took a deep breath, pictured herself standing there in Lilly's red dress with hair and makeup done and perfume at her neck, knees, wrists, and thighs. "I'm here. Of course I'm here. I was just trying to take it all in, all that you said. You did the same thing last night, said everything you wanted to say all at once, and it takes me a moment to figure it all out. That's all. But I'm here."

"Rose. I'm glad that you're there. Can I . . . ? Will you let me . . . ? See you . . . ?"

Cookie was practically jumping out of her skin, mouth and eyes smiling and laughing and sly, like she and Rose were the same people, Goddesses, and it made nothing but sense for random men to fall at their feet.

Some of Cookie's confidence and brittle sweetness

rubbed off on Rose and she said, "Okay. All right. I'll see you again."

"Today?"

Rose thought about having to go home and explain to Mama that she had some sort of date with a man that she'd met in a bar that she wasn't supposed to be in the night before and she was going but don't worry because she would do all her homework before school on Monday.

"Okay. I can see you today." Rose was thinking about the time that she had to rearrange, the lies that she had to tell, and Cookie was silently cheering her on, giving her the thumbs-up sign like the whole thing was a team effort.

"When? At what time? Where?"

"I don't know. Maybe a late lunch somewhere downtown?"

"I know a place. Do you want me to come get you?"

Cookie frantically shaking her head and Rose could just imagine all the hell that would break loose if some random long-limbed man with eyes like morning who didn't even belong in North Philly just showed up at Cookie's house. "It's better, I mean I think that I would be more comfortable if I met you somewhere. Do you know a place?"

"You want to go downtown, right? Let me think. There's a really nice place on Chestnut Street. The food and service are good, and it's small and I think that we can sit down and talk to each other. What time is good for you?"

"How about three o'clock?"

"Three o'clock sounds good."

Charles gave Rose the address and they hung up the phone and Rose and Cookie just stood staring at each other.

Cookie said, "Girl, you so bad I'm scared of you."

Rose stared at the child's face on the cereal box, the wide smile, white teeth, and light eyes. She wasn't feeling dangerous and almost grown. She was almost eighteen but she was still a little girl playing with dolls and sculpting women. "Cookie, I only know one thing about him. That one thing. I can't even remember what he looked liked, really, besides for that."

"Well, why did you give him this number if you didn't want him to call here?"

"I didn't think he would call and you were sitting there with that man and . . . I don't know."

"Go out with him. I kind of remember what he looked like. He was cute, Rose. What's his name?"

Cookie was back at the table, shoving soggy cereal in her mouth, her short white nightgown in her lap so that her flowered panties were showing.

"His name's Charles. Cookie, you saying you would go?"

Cookie was getting impatient. "Isn't that what you just told him? That you were going to go?"

"I said that but that doesn't mean that I have to show up."

"Okay. You're meeting him in a restaurant, all these people will be around you. I think he was kind of cute and he looked young. And the things he said on the phone, Rose. I never had anyone say those things to me. Aren't you curious? Seriously, aren't you just a bit curious? If I were you I would go, Rose. I would go just to see."

Rose was almost persuaded by Cookie's wisdom. "You think so?"

Cookie nodded her head, poured more cereal into her

bowl, and added milk. "I do. I really think so. What's the absolute worst thing that could happen?"

She went to meet Charles at the restaurant at three o'clock. Called Mama before leaving Cookie's house and told her that she was going to stay with Cookie's family for Sunday dinner and she would be home by six. Cookie dressed her in a long sleeveless yellow dress from her closet. Rose sat quietly on the edge of Cookie's bed while Cookie put her hair up in a large ponytail at the center of her head and used the hot curlers to add bends and waves. Cookie put lipstick on her mouth and a little blush on her cheeks and perfume at her wrists and neck.

Rose left Cookie's house a shining and sweet-smelling thing and it was late April and wearing Cookie's yellow dress she was simply another color of spring. She rode the subway downtown and people stared at her wondering where she was going and who she was going to meet and she had no idea.

Studio Time

WOOD AND STONE AND FLESH, flesh and stone and wood, all of it coming together like Earth and sky after God said let there be light or the Big Bang rocked the Universe, rocked and shifted and changed so that nothing was ever the same again, could never be the same because there was no going back just moving forward in gasping, painful motions. Moving forward with blood on the hands and blood clouding the vision and blood dripping from between open thighs, digging for the beauty.

She sat, hands, a woman's long fingers shaving the insides and the outsides of inanimate objects that were, nonetheless, breathing, crying out as bits and pieces and slivers and dust fell to the floor at her feet. And remembering Mama sitting next to her on the small width of her childhood bed with her belly sticking out and round, in the room that she shared with her sister who was running the streets sucking death in through the body, Mama telling her, "All you have to do is let it all go, let it all go and start over. You left and now you home and home is a place of beginnings." Mama sitting and talking to her night after night in the dark and the stillness, the only concrete thing that she had to hold on to, besides the roundness of her belly, the shape and outline of her child. Mama talking to her at night and she working frantically in the basement during the day, hands sculpting wood and stone trying to form a woman so full of pain and fright that her eyes couldn't look outward, could only look inward, stay subdued and quiet.

Working, hands flexing and fingers searching, and during breaks heading for the closets, the space beneath beds and the room behind the kitchen, the itch of the old rug beneath the dining room table. Spaces big enough to hide her and the belly, big enough yet out of sight and safe for her and her child. She was sitting under the dining room table, long lace tablecloth hiding her from view, sipping tea and eating Mama's oatmeal cookies, comfortable and breath easy but choking on the tea and cookies when she realized, all at once, that she needed to stop hiding. Stop hiding because there wasn't any hiding place.

No hiding place and spring of 1968 and no one who looked like her talking about the vote or integration or wanting to be liked and accepted, admitted to all those places that still, despite the Civil Rights Movement, had NO ADMITTANCE signs. Everyone who looked like her talking about breaking down doors, taking over schools, power and liberation. She wanted to be strong like that even though mostly men did all the talking. She wanted to be strong and make strong or vulnerable or sad or peaceful women who already knew what she was just learning.

The end of a decade, the death of heroes with faces like hers, free love practiced with casual cruelty so that a boy she loved could whisper "beautiful black cunt" while between her thighs, an intellectual redefinition of ugliness to make it sweet, terms of endearment that crushed her chest and made pleasure and response impossible.

No immediate action came begging at the heels of realization. For days, weeks, she went to all her hiding places, took tea and cookies and books and sketch pads, and just sat there trying to visualize and draw whole women who weren't damaged, confined to smallness. From each sheet of paper in her sketch pad women with her dull eyes and her unhappy mouth stared back at her. There were pictures of women scattered beneath the dining room table, pictures of women huddled beneath the beds, pictures of women hanging like clothes from hooks in the closets.

The roundness of her belly, the exuberant movements of her child kept her grounded; her child was the good, the focus, all that she needed as free love withered and died and almost everyone, except people talking power and liberation and taking over, went back to the places they came from and forgot. Went back to their black parents and black communities living in the rural South or fast-paced Northern cities. Went back to their white parents in the midwest on farms or living happily and blindly in the suburbs. The child inside her kept her from withering, kept her from forgetting, kept her fighting as free love faded into Black Power.

The first labor pains sent her scurrying from beneath the dining room table, cookies and tea leaving crumbs and wet behind her. On her hands and knees crawling and hearing her sister, Lilly, stoned almost out of her mind, scream, "Black Power!" Scream it just like that, alone, with no lead-in and no context and getting down on all fours to crawl and meet her in the middle of the floor and gather her in her arms as another contraction hit. Lilly rocked her and rocked her and kept whispering "Black Power, Black Power" like a nursery rhyme and she concentrated on those two words. She had heard them before, was all the time listening for them, but she never heard them with such force or determination, never by her sister smelling like some man's sex and kissing the side of her neck, massaging the small of her back. Lilly dressed in her dashiki and sprouting locks and gathering her in, helping her to bear her own weight and so high that she couldn't say anything else, couldn't ask, "How are you? You hurt? What you need me to do?" could only offer those two words. Black Power in Lilly's arm, coming from Lilly's mouth and the words becoming something else, something different than what she always thought they meant, from what brothers on television and brothers marching and brothers taking over and finding manhood or redefining black manhood meant. Lilly making Black Power specific and intimate, Lilly making Black Power about soft arms and soft breasts and warm, scented bodies and strength, strength in the middle of all that softness or maybe strength because of all that softness and the hardness beneath the softness always there. Lilly making

Black Power her sisters and Mama and sculpting women and raising a child, community of women and Black Power like benediction falling over all of them.

Rose focused on the words instead of the pain, played with them in her head, took them apart to examine them separately. BLACK. Black like the earth, warm and alive with green things growing. Black like Mama's skin, Mama's hands with ringed fingers and soft palms. Black like the deepest, darkest wood, too expensive for her to work on all the time, but giving off a perfect shine, a perfect light. Black like the child she carried inside of her. Black like bodies hanging from trees with the sex and head chopped off and whole towns gathered around like cruelty was really a festival in disguise.

POWER. Power like being terrified, being terrorized and still keeping moving. Power like the love Mama and her sisters always gave her, with no expectations and lots of dreams. Power like watching black children being sprayed with fire hoses and still fighting. Power like shaping women from wood and stone and flesh and blood. Power like the child in her belly roaring to get out.

She started chanting with Lilly in between contractions, "Black Power, Black Power, Black Power . . ."

It was like a prayer, a mantra, and the child in her belly grew calm, the force of the contractions lessened, the tension slowly left her body even as Lilly kept massaging her lower back and raining scattered kisses across her face. Lilly holding her and Lilly giving her something precious so she felt that they were little girls again, sharing secrets and clothes and the same room, twins separated at birth, wandering and lost, by chance finding each other.

That was how her sister, Violet, who took her to the hospital and waited out the birth with her, found them. Sitting on the floor, wrapped in each other, Black Power falling like caresses from their lips.

Imani

I MANI WAS THE DAUGHTER of a father she had never known. Mommy had lovers, plenty of lovers who stayed nights and were at the breakfast table sipping herbal tea when she awoke for school. Mommy was still in bed, because Mommy didn't get up before ten in the morning any day. Imani joined them, these men who had slept in Mommy's bed the night before. They made her tea and wheat toast and oatmeal with honey. They were usually big and black and kind and they asked her about school and painted pictures of all the places that they had been— Ghana, Kenya, Brazil, Argentina, Colombia. Places far away where just about everyone was brown and looked like her.

She carved out pictures of her father, of what she thought her father was, from the hands and knees and kindness of the men who slept in Mommy's bed at night. Her father was perhaps tall and broad-shouldered. He had locks that fell to his waist and hands that put her hair up in whatever way she desired. Hands that made her breakfast, hands that she held on the way to school, hands that never hurt.

If it were a weekend then she and Mommy's lover fixed Mommy tea and took it up to her. Sometimes Mommy's lover would give Imani a piggyback up the stairs. The walls in Mommy's room red and covered in cloth with pictures of black and brown women carrying baskets on their heads and smiling. There was a dresser and a vanity table with a mirror and makeup and perfume scattered atop the surface. Mommy's lover put the tea on the dresser and then they jumped in bed and shook Mommy, and they all rolled about together. Mommy woke up laughing, and holding Imani and holding her lover and holding herself. Mommy smelled like roses, like the house smelled like roses because she was always burning incense and telling Imani not to touch it because it would hurt her. Mommy's braids were long and thick and when she took them out her hair took up all the space. Mommy was dark, darker than Imani. She wanted to look like Mommy, to have that hair and that dark skin that was so soft and pretty and always smelled of roses, like the house, red like the bedroom of Mommy's walls.

Imani lived in a place where all the walls were brightly colored. Mommy worked with wood and stone and her hands were always cut and sometimes bleeding. Mommy made shapes and people, mostly women. Women with round, lush figures and laughing faces, women who danced and sang and sat and sometimes stood straight looking grim and sad or maybe serious and strong. Mommy's women lived and breathed in the house, although Imani realized that they weren't really like people, they didn't have hearts that beat or blood that pumped but she was sure that they felt things, saw things and just didn't tell.

Imani had her own room. A room that was little and yellow and comfortable. There were pillows everywhere, no chairs, and black dolls stared at her with faces like her own.

Saturday mornings after tea in bed, and Mommy holding Imani and her lover at the same time, and watching cartoons because Imani liked them, Mommy turned to her lover and said, "Okay, sweetheart, you need to go. I spend Saturday with my child."

If it was a man Imani really liked, one who made her really good oatmeal and put extra honey on it, she'd ask Mommy if he could stay. Mommy let him because Saturday was Imani's day. Most of the time it was just her and Mommy. Mommy walked her lover to the door and came laughing back to Imani, and then she'd stop and bite her lip uncertainly. "You like him, don't you?" she'd ask.

"Yes, I like him," Imani said.

Mommy gathered her up and placed her on her lap. "I mean, you don't dislike the fact that he comes over sometimes? Or the others? They're Mommy's friends, and Mommy wants you to like her friends."

Imani played with the hem of Mommy's nightgown, growing a bit bored with the conversation. "I like it when they come over. They cook and do my hair and we laugh and laugh and wake you up in the mornings."

"All right, love. What do you want to do today?"

Saturdays were for walking. They lived in a neighborhood where people looked liked them. There were lots of children, children who played hide-and-seek between the cars parked on their small block. Imani had lots of friends. She liked to jump double Dutch, and play jacks and Mommy sometimes let her have sleepovers Saturday nights with all her girlfriends. Her girlfriends walked her to school in the morning and sneaked her candy because Mommy usually didn't allow her to have it.

On Saturdays she and Mommy left their neighborhood. They caught the bus at the corner of their block and they went downtown. Downtown there were all kinds of different people. People who looked like her and people who didn't look like her. People who were pale with yellow and red and black hair that hung straight down their backs; people whose eyes were blue and gray and hazel and green; people who talked different and smiled different and laughed different.

They went out to lunch and Mommy made her read the menu and tell the waitress her order. It was a Mexican restaurant because Imani loved spicy food. Mommy ordered a margarita. Imani said, "Oh, Mommy, could I have one of those, too?"

"Sure. Can you bring her a virgin margarita in a small glass?"

The waitress was pale and blond and green-eyed. "Of course I can. She's such a pretty little girl."

Imani smiled because pretty was important.

The waitress left and Mommy said, "Hey, baby. You are pretty on the outside, just like that woman said. But being pretty on the outside doesn't mean much."

"How come?"

Mommy shrugged and ran her hands over the wildness of

her head. Her hair didn't fall straight down her back, it stood all over the place and Imani wanted hair like that. "Let's see. Um, you don't have to work at pretty. You just are usually and it has nothing to do with you, really. It's like you lucked out and for no reason. Like . . . It's like when you put your foot in the circle to decide who's in a game of tag. Someone has to be it, but it isn't because of something they did good or bad, it's just because someone has to be."

"Oh. Pretty just is?"

"Yeah, pretty just is. That's all."

The food came and it was hot and spicy and Imani took a bite and burned her tongue. Tears came and she pushed her plate away, waiting for the food to cool, the steam making her neck and face damp.

Mommy said, "All right?"

She nodded. "It's just that it's real real hot, is all."

The restaurant was crowded and loud, all the sound echoing off the walls, off floors, off plates and glasses and people. The walls were cream and yellow, boring walls.

They ate quickly and went back to the streets, holding hands because the confusion of downtown sometimes frightened Imani and Mommy was always worried that she'd get lost, or that someone might snatch her. They stopped at jewelry shops because Mommy liked bright shiny things, wore them in her ears, on her neck, wrists, and ankles.

They went to toy stores because Imani liked toys, liked the silly stuffed dolls, the puzzles, and the trucks. Mommy let her get one toy each Saturday, and she wandered the aisles carefully, testing out this or that truck, holding and shaking this or that doll. It was a hard thing to be in a toy store and have to pick a toy. It wasn't the same as Christmas or her birthday; then she just woke up and the toys were there—all she had to do was play with them. Sometimes she picked a truck because it was red and moved fast when she rolled it on the floor and she could put stuff in it. Sometimes she picked a doll because it was black and she could braid her hair and put clothes on her and pretend that she was real.

Most Saturdays they went to the Franklin Institute Science Museum, because Imani loved and was terrified of The Heart all at once. The first time Mommy took her there she could only stare, amazed that there existed a heart somewhere in the world that was the size of a house—a heart that she could walk through and hear the beating and the roar of blood rushing to a body that didn't exist. It was the lack of a body that terrified Imani, even though Mommy explained that it wasn't really a heart, just something made by men. But how could anyone make a heart without a body? There was no sense in it.

Walking through The Heart was like walking through a red cave, like the Hell that Grandma believed in. Imani made Mommy keep her hands on her shoulders, she didn't want to fall on the steps or lean against the smooth red walls that she could hear beating. The walls that had small holes and lines and puzzles, walls that looked like the inside of her, holding her breath in a heart like the heart hiding beneath her shirt, beneath the skin and bones and tissue.

Saturdays when they came home the block was alive. No more pale people with blond and red and black straight hair. On their block were people who looked like her and talked like her and laughed like her. Imani didn't understand why she and Mommy and the people who looked like them were called black because none of them were. They were all shades of brown and yellow and red and cream; some had hair that hung straight down their backs, but most had hair like Mommy—hair that stood straight up, hair that took up space and didn't apologize for it. Some were small and quiet; others were large and loud. Most of the women were round and brown or round and yellow or round and red and lovely. Imani liked their loveliness because it was like Mommy and Mommy's women, but most of the time she stared into the faces of the men.

She was the daughter of a father she had never seen, would never see. Any man walking along the street could be her father. He could be Mr. Sam at the candy store who sometimes gave her free gum and soda after school, or Mr. Willie who was always sitting at the stump on his corner, or Mr. Keith who was married and had three kids. The picture that she had of him, which she had painstakingly pieced together from the collage of Mommy's lovers, was constantly changing, shifting, rearranging itself. Sometimes he, the father that she had never seen, was light, sometimes dark. Sometimes he had a large Afro, sometimes he had locks, sometimes he had no hair at all. Sometimes he was short and thin or thin and tall or fat and short. Sometimes he was smiling or frowning or crying because he had a daughter with no face like The Heart had no body.

Studio Time

THE SKY OUTSIDE OF HER WINDOW was immense, and blue, and the sun resembled a child's ball in roundness and the color of full, large sunflowers but no dark at the center. She sat cross-legged on the floor, carefully sketching a woman and a girl child, standing close so that the head of the child rested in the curve of the woman's full waist. Beautiful girl child, sketch loosely based upon Imani, braids and smiles and a lightness that came through the eyes, that spread out from the fingertips gathered in front of her chest, resting lightly against her brown skin. She was going to sculpt the sketch in wood, dark expensive wood that would give off a rich, impervious shine.

Her child, Imani, still a little girl and trying so hard to grow up, to rush that walk to womanhood that was slow for a reason. Little woman child, and it was no easy thing. No easy thing at all even though she was trying to make it as seamless as possible, no major breaks, no unseen trauma, just falling into womanhood gracefully, with laughter instead of tears in the heart.

The woman and child were taking on a definite shape beneath her hand. The woman was very round, big-breasted, big-hipped, and legs that were long and strong and sturdy to the ground. Skirts billowed out at her feet and a blouse clung to her upper body and her hair was in a huge Afro on top of the head. The child was small, about seven or eight years old, Imani's age. Her limbs were long and slender and fragile. Her eyes were huge and there was a shy smile playing about her mouth, hands gathered at her chest and head resting against the woman.

She remembered the night she crawled from beneath the dining room table at her mother's house and into Lilly's arms, remembered Violet finding them down on the floor chanting Black Power. Violet pried her away from Lilly, cursing up a storm and her hair flying about her head because Lilly refused to let go of Rose. The more Violet pulled and cursed the tighter Lilly held. Lilly whispered, "Faith. Imani," and Rose held on to the words, held on to them because they were a gift too precious to be discarded. Violet finally managed to get her away from Lilly and being ripped out of Lilly's arm was excruciating, another contraction.

Her clothes were wet from her and Lilly's sweat and sometime while they were lying there her water had broken and there was a small puddle on the floor and Lilly was just sitting in it. Violet placed one arm across her shoulders, the other across her back and hauled her to Daddy's old leather chair, sat her down and told her to shut up, and not to move as if she could, as if she had any plans on going anywhere. She couldn't stop saying "Black Power," saying it over and over again, saying it through her breathing and through the pain. Lilly sitting in birthing fluids from Rose's body and chanting Black Power even as Violet lifted her small, wasted form out of the wet, retrieved a mop from the kitchen, and cleaned the floor.

Violet took her to the hospital, leaving Lilly standing in the middle of the floor, eyes glazed, staring after them. Violet rushing her to the car, pushing her in and behind the driver's seat and all she could do was rest her head against the cool window and keep chanting. Violet started the car, asked, "Does that help?" And she frantically nodded and tried to focus all her attention on the rhythmic pattern trailing from her panting body.

The ride to the hospital was extremely short, Violet passing cars and beeping her horn effortlessly, hair blowing, and all the time keeping up endless chatter. "I swear to God, when I walked in and saw the two of you laying on the floor my heart almost stopped. I kept telling Jerome that something was wrong, just this feeling I had. I tried calling first but no one answered and I knew Mama was at work and Lilly probably fucked up and I was so worried about you. Then to walk in the door and see you both sitting there in the middle of all that mess and sweating and mumbling about Black Power like it was a lifeline, like if only you both kept saying that everything would be all right. And nobody calling the doctor, or an ambulance, or making any kind of attempt to get you anywhere near a hospital. I could kill you, I could kill you both."

At the hospital time slowed down, slowed down until they were almost sleepwalking. Her belly was constantly shifting and rolling, it felt as if the baby were trying to pull out her insides, as if it would kill her if it needed to in order to get out. She was amazed by such single-minded determination, such a ferocious sense of purpose.

Violet brought her crushed ice to chew on, rubbed her lower back, and held her hand as they rolled her down to the delivery room. Violet's presence lessened the embarrassment when doctors and nurses spread her legs and gathered between them, their touch cold against her flesh. Violet was there to scream with her, and coach her through her breathing, and help her keep up the chant of Black Power even as doctors and nurses glanced at them nervously, smiled politely. She needed Violet because her body was no longer her body, it belonged to her huge belly, and the child, her child trying to get out. She wanted to close her legs, squeeze the walls of her vagina tight in order not to let this thing happen, there was panic as she considered what having a child meant, what having a child would make her. She stopped breathing and almost blacked out but Violet was there, holding her hand so tightly that her fingers were crushed and screaming at her, "Take a deep breath, a deep breath and let it all go, baby. Let it all go."

She was sobbing now, almost hysterical, and Violet was screaming at her, wouldn't stop screaming at her and her body was tired of fighting. She relaxed, took a deep breath, and pushed it all out of her. She felt it start at the very top of her brain, lingering just beneath the skin of her scalp and making its way down, down through the tenseness of her neck and shoulders, down through the frantic beating of her heart, down through the laboring gasps of her lungs, down through the rolling emptiness of her stomach and the crushing pain in her lower back, down into the uterus, where the child was scrambling desperately about searching for an out. She felt the child moving through her, being pushed through her cervix and her vaginal canal and being thrown into the light—harsh, brilliant, artificial light—and men and women in sterile white coats staring down at it.

Violet said, "It's a girl, Rose. A girl and she is so beautiful." Violet was crying, she never cried, but her nose was running and her makeup was messed about her face.

The doctors placed the girl child on her stomach, quiet now, no longer ferocious but still and at peace, staring up at her with huge eyes.

"What's her name?" a nurse asked and she remembered the gift that Lilly had given her.

"Imani. Imani for faith," she said and ran her fingers over her daughter's scalp.

"That's pretty, Rose. How did you come up with it?" Violet asked.

"Lilly. Lilly gave it to me." She lay there with her child at her breast and her sister beside her and the name of her other sister in the air. She thought of Black Power.

BLACK POWER. Black Power was like giving birth to a girl child and at the same exact moment giving birth to a new self.

Phone
Conversation

"MAMA? Mama, beautiful Mama, one I love . . ."

"Oh, God. Lilly? Where are you, baby? It's been over two weeks and I just want to know where you are."

"Mama, it doesn't matter. I can be in Mozambique fighting the Portuguese or Brazil living on the street or here in North Philly fighting the police."

"I don't understand why you do this, Lilly. I didn't know that dreaming was all that you could do until it was too late and you were this grown woman still spinning little-girl fantasies and getting high to hold on to it all."

"Mama, love, I'm not a little girl. Believe me, I know."

"Tell me where you are and I'll come get you and bring you home."

"Didn't I say I could be anywhere, Mama? It really doesn't matter, the same shit would still be happening to me, to all of us."

"Oh, Lilly . . ."

"Did I tell you that I could be in Africa right now? Right

now at this very moment calling you long-distance just to say hello."

"Baby, you talk like you're Imani and eight years old and surrounded by dolls and nothing to do besides play make-believe."

"Calling from Africa and staying with my African prince and he is good to me like Daddy was good to me."

"Lilly, what did I do wrong? How did I fail you? Because in the end it's always the mother's fault or the mother's glory or the mother's pride."

"Mama, do you want to know his name?"

"Lilly, just tell me what I need to do to help you. I think about it and think about it and . . . Lilly, I don't know how long I can keep doing this."

"His name is Salah and—"

"The phone calls in the middle of the night . . ."

"And I'm his first wife. His first love, really—"

"Every time you walk out the house not being sure when you coming back or even if you coming back at all . . ."

"He really wants me to be happy . . ."

"The lying and the stealing and—"

"He tells me I'm beautiful every day, Mama . . ."

"Like I'm watching my child fade away and there's nothing I can do . . . You are killing yourself, baby. Killing yourself and asking everyone else to just stand around and watch."

"Don't you worry, Mama. He's going to take care of me. I'll be fine."

"Tell me how to get to you so that I can bring you home."

"Home, Mama? You'll take me home?"

"Of course I will. Listen, stop crying. Don't cry. Just tell me, Lilly."

Operator: "Please deposit ten cents."

"Lilly, do you have any more change?"

"I don't have anything, Mama. I don't have anything at all."

Studio Time

THE CHISEL ATE SOFTLY AT THE STONE, chipped away lightly, so there were no shards just dust at her feet, dust floating in the air like fog on a cloudy day. She kept a cloth mask over her face and nose so she wouldn't breathe it in, wouldn't have stone particles stubbornly clinging to her nostrils and throat and lungs. Making a woman, slender and strong and angry. So angry, anger humming just beneath her facial expression and making the outline of her body tense and fierce. No jewels, no adornments, and hair braided simple and close to the scalp to keep it out of the way. No skirts, skirts weren't practical, just slim pants that couldn't be grabbed at or held on to, pants that wouldn't slow her down. A top that fit her body like a second skin, a top that she could move in, use her torso and chest and arms to hurt or get away.

She had known women like that, used to see them sometimes when she attended Black Panther meetings, although most women were quiet at the meetings. Seen them more often once black women got involved with Women's Liberation and all the time keeping score of every insult, every way in which they were left out, stilled, hushed.

Lilly took her to her first Panther meeting. She knew all about Black Power, all the time reading about Black Liberation, all the time opening her home and her arms and her legs for any black man talking black politics and looking to be held. She wanted that strength, what she saw as strength and no need for hiding places and she was trying to get rid of the guilt, get rid of the places she had been while people with faces like hers were fighting and marching and being killed from sea to shining sea.

Late spring of 1971 and Philly trying to settle itself down, trying not to think about the long hot summer ahead and how summer was the time when people lost their patience and tempers and burned things down. She was still staying at Mama's, and next-door neighbors sitting on their porches until late evening sipping iced tea or lemonade laced with a little corn liquor and eating crabs or clams on newspaper on cement stoops. Little girls jumping double Dutch and little boys riding bikes and waiting for school to close.

Lilly was trying to clean herself up then, had gained weight and the bruises had started to fade from her arms, and she was wearing skirts and soft blouses and looking like she did before she started staying out all night and coming home not being able to put two words together. Lilly was even starting to write again, beautiful poetry that made Rose wonder over the interior of Lilly's life, the life that took place in run-down houses and back alleys while she was shooting up.

Lilly was better and attending Black Panther meetings and talking about revolution but not about death, Lilly couldn't kill anyone. Rose wanted so badly to believe that Lilly had beaten whatever had gotten hold of her that when Lilly invited her to a Party meeting she accepted. She always wanted to go but never had the time between Imani and job and sculpting women. Mama was at work and Violet was at swim lessons with Kevin and Keith and there was no baby-sitter, certainly no one she trusted enough to leave her three-year-old daughter with. Lilly just shrugged and said, "We'll take Imani with us."

Rose strapped Imani in the stroller and they left the house, heading out to West Philly.

They had to catch the subway from North Philly to Center City, and then the trolley out into West Philly. It was about a forty-five-minute ride and Lilly held the baby bag, talking like she was trying to make up for being completely out of it for so long, hands nervously and frantically moving. "I know I was fucked up, no one knows better than me how absolutely fucked up I was. Maybe Mama but that's because she loves me so hard, stayed up nights and cleaned up blood and all kinds of nastiness from the bathroom floor, from around the toilet seat. I remember laying there one night—this was when you were still living on South Street—so high that I could feel my heartbeat slowing down, watching Mama clean up the mess I made. She was crying, Rose. I can count on my hand the number of times that I've seen Mama cry. There she was, on her hands and knees for me, crying like it was killing her, like I was killing her, and I wished that I was dead. I wished that she would reach over and finish the job that I had already started. Just finish it because we both were exhausted, just tired and there was no end in sight. I knew that if she didn't kill me when I came down or got off I'd start searching for my next hit and we'd be back in the bathroom in the middle of the night, back at the same place that we started.

"And sure enough, nothing happened, and we kept repeating the same cycle, over and over. Me getting high and coming home to her so that she could clean up my shit. Sometimes I tried to recite some of my poetry to her, you know, to kind of give her something for being so good to me, but that just made her cry harder. Cry harder even as I was telling her, fucked up out of my head, how lovely she was, and what a terrific thing it was to be a strong black woman, and how blessed I was to have a strong black mother. Saying all of this while she's down on all fours like she's my maid. My maid. So that's what I started to pretend that she was. It was easier, easier to imagine that I was Scarlett O'Hara or some other languid white girl and she was working for me. Anything was easier than her being my mother cleaning up my shit and blood and vomit. Anything.

"I thought that we would go on like that forever, and it didn't even bother me. Nothing bothered me unless I couldn't get high and then my whole life felt like trash that I didn't want and couldn't throw out. Then Mama surprised me. The middle of the night and we were in our endlessly reoccurring roles, she was down on her knees scrubbing and crying and I was laying with my cheek against the tiles of the bathroom floor watching her when something just broke inside of her. Just broke so that she threw the rag that she was cleaning with at me, threw it at me hard so that it hit me in the face, disinfectant burning my eyes, dirty water drifting down my cheeks like tears, and I could only stare at her, could only stare at her and think nobody ever threw shit at Scarlett.

"Mama came at me, got up and walked over to me and squatted down by my side. She was so angry and so tired and I felt her wet hands moving across my shoulders and settling on my throat, just resting there lightly. I swear, I thought she was going to kill me. It was there in her eyes or nothing was in her eyes and that nothing told me that she was capable of anything. I wanted her to do it, started praying for her to just do it and be done and we would never live through another night like this one again. That was the only thing that mattered, never living through another night like all the nights that had passed. Mama's hands were tightening slowly around my throat and she was humming softly under her breath like she used to when we were kids to put us to sleep, and I could feel all the air leaving my body, being pulled out of me by Mama's hands. That's when I became scared. I tried to get away, but Mama's hands just kept tightening and she started to hum louder and louder and I was sobbing, crying and grabbing at her fingers and finally I managed to get out, 'Please, Mama . . .' She pulled back and stared at her hands for a long time and then stared at me laying on the floor sobbing and nose running and bruises lining my arms. She said, 'The next time I come in here and have to clean up after you I will kill you. Believe me, Lilly. I will.' She said it calm, no hollering or screaming, and she

left, just stepped right over me and left. I never felt so abandoned in my entire life. That's when I knew I had to try to
get things back under control. I'm trying, I'm trying so hard
because I want Mama back, and I don't want to be a motherless child. There's no way that I could survive that."

Rose was still reeling from the image of Mama trying to
kill Lilly in the bathroom when they arrived at the Black
Panther meeting. She was still trying to take it all in and see
her mother's long, dark fingers wrapped around the yellow
of Lilly's long neck. Mama killing a grown child who didn't
want to be grown, killing a grown child so that she wouldn't
have to scamper behind her with wet rag in hand.

The meeting was in someone's house, big spacious row
house with a front and backyard and trees lining a quiet
block. Quiet block near the University of Pennsylvania and
trees and grass and green and she had never really been out
to this part of West Philly before, all the houses three stories
and huge and old. The inside of the house was beautiful,
hardwood floors and African prints hanging on the walls.
Men and women dressed primarily in black seated in chairs,
at tables, sprawled out across the floor.

Rose settled herself in a chair that one of the women had
fetched for her after noticing, with some surprise, that she
had brought Imani. Lilly knew almost everyone and smiled
and laughed and glided across the room, looking like a
dancer or a spirit woman. Rose held a sleepy Imani on her
lap and watched as men grabbed Lilly's arms, touched her
hair, ran fingers up and down her back, patted her on the
ass, whispered in her ear. Brothers doing all of the talking
while women wandered in and out of their small groups.

Rose sat there holding her child and thinking about the limitations of Black Power, why she was all the time creating women and daughters in her studio. All the time creating a community of women because in her community, community of people with faces like hers, community of people all the time talking about and fighting over Black Power and Black Liberation, there was little space for her, for any her.

Imani

T HE SUNLIGHT FROM THE WINDOW just above her bed directly in her face, hot on her even though it was growing cold outside. The door of Mommy's room opened and Imani listened as Mommy crossed the hall and knocked on her door.

Mommy came in wearing her long green nightgown that looked like a really pretty dress. Imani held out her arms and Mommy came and crawled into her small bed with her.

"Good morning, baby," Mommy said.

Imani held her or tried to and laughed. "My arms can't even go around you."

"Then I'll hold you." Mommy shifted her until she was lying with her head on Mommy's breasts.

She played with the ends of Mommy's braids. "We still going over to Grandma's today?"

"Yup."

"Everyone will be there?"

"I think so."

"Even Aunt Lilly? I haven't seen her in a while." Aunt Lilly was always humming or singing or telling stories and wishing on stars and trees and birds in flight for good luck.

"Mama said she's going to be there. So I guess she will. I hope so."

Imani lay quiet, thinking about Grandma and Aunt Lilly and Aunt Violet.

"I think I'm going to cook breakfast. What you want?" Mommy asked.

"We got kiwi?"

"Yes, I think so."

"Then I want kiwi and grits."

"No eggs and pancakes?"

"No."

"Okay." Mommy jumped out of bed and Imani watched as her green nightgown lifted and settled about her.

Mommy left and Imani's pillow smelled like roses and peppermint and the space on the bed where Mommy had lain was warm. Imani rolled into that space and pulled the covers over her head, keeping in the scent. She sang one of Mommy's freedom songs. It was Aunt Lilly who told her about the bus boycott. Aunt Lilly who told the story so that it almost seemed like Imani was there when a whole bunch of people who looked like her and talked like her walked instead of riding the bus with heads held down.

Imani only saw Aunt Lilly really angry once, and that was last year when she was only seven and not quite a big girl. Mommy was out of town at an art show and Aunt Lilly was baby-sitting her. Aunt Lilly wanted to take her over to her boyfriend's house. She gave her a bath because she was out all day playing with the children on Grandma's block and Aunt Lilly said that she smelled and there was no way that she was taking any child who smelled like that with her anywhere.

They left the house and it was late afternoon, summertime, and the sun was big and round.

"Where does he live?" Imani asked, grabbing hold of Aunt Lilly's hand.

"Not far. Around the corner. And his name is Bryan."

"I like that name. Bryan. Is he nice?"

"Yeah, he's nice. But more than that, he's strong and proud and fierce. He's a Black Panther, Imani."

"Like the big cat?"

"Named after the cat because he's a fighter."

"Okay. What does he do?"

Aunt Lilly stopped and bent down to her. "He fights for all the people who look and talk and act like you and me. Our people, Imani. Our people."

Imani was quiet, thinking it all over. A Black Panther who wasn't a cat and didn't live in the jungle and didn't really eat people or animals, but a fighter for all the people who looked like her. She wasn't sure what that meant, and she didn't want to ask Aunt Lilly again because she was humming to herself and had that faraway look in her eyes, like she was going or gone. Aunt Lilly told her that sometimes she went to a private place in her head, a place where everything made sense and she didn't have to figure out or discover or fight, all she had to do was be and drift and listen to the music of her insides. Imani wondered what that music sounded like; tried to place the tune that Aunt Lilly was humming softly. It was alien and mysterious and beautiful and Imani wanted the music of her insides to sound like that, to sound like something because when she listened to herself there was no music at all.

"Bryan live with his mama like you live with Grandma?"

Aunt Lilly quit humming and smiled down at her. "No, he lives with his comrades."

"His who?"

"His comrades. Other Black Panthers who are his friends."

"Oh."

The house that Bryan lived in looked just like the house that Grandma lived in, a two-story brick row home with a stoop. The only difference was that Grandma's front door was brown all over and Bryan's door was painted in colors of green and yellow and red and black.

"How come his door looks like that?" Imani asked, as Aunt Lilly put on lip gloss and knocked.

"The colors of Africa, baby."

"Africa where we from?" Mommy had told her all about the Atlantic Ocean and the land that was everyone's first home.

"Yeah."

"Then how come Grandma or Mommy or anybody else don't have their doors painted like that? If we all from Africa?"

A huge man opened the door, tall and thick but not fat. He was bald. Imani had never seen anyone who had absolutely no hair at all. Did he shave it all off or did it just fall out for no special reason? He was brown, bleeding into yellow, and his eyes were light, light brown. First thing he did was grab Aunt Lilly and kiss her like he was happy to see her.

"Hey," he said, still holding Aunt Lilly and then smiling down at Imani. "And who is this?"

His voice was slow like he had all the time in the world to say what he needed to say and no one and nobody was going to rush him. Imani was charmed. "Where are you from?" she asked, trying to picture a place where everyone talked like that, lazy and deliberate.

Bryan laughed. "Georgia. What's your name, honey?"

The way he said honey had Imani straightening her back and smiling her widest smile. "Imani. Rose is my mommy."

"Why don't you all come on in out of the sun and all?"

The house inside was dark and cool, walls of different shades of brown and pictures and paintings of black people everywhere. Music was everywhere, music that almost sounded like church music but wasn't quite because church music never talked about men leaving and men cheating and men breaking hearts.

Bryan sat Imani down on the floor, but she didn't mind because there were fat, plush pillows everywhere—yellow and red and bright, bright blue. Aunt Lilly and Bryan went into the kitchen, leaving her alone. She stretched out and looked up at the smooth brown ceiling and played with the round earrings dangling against her neck.

Imani didn't even hear him come down the stairs, just felt this presence in the room with her and slowly sat up and found him sitting cross-legged on the floor a good distance away from her. "Hello. I'm Imani." He had more hair than anyone that she had ever seen, probably had more hair than anyone else in the entire world. It was locked, like Aunt Lilly's, and fell down his back like water to form a puddle around him. He was dark, skin so dark and smooth and pretty that he seemed to steal all the light in the room and give it back with more of a glow.

"Hi, Imani. I'm Taji." He smiled and his teeth were white and slightly crooked.

His voice wasn't slow, lazy like Bryan's, but the words still impossibly deliberate. "Where are you from?" She had never realized that there were a million different ways of saying exactly the same thing.

"New York. What about you?"

"I'm from here."

"Really? And how old are you?"

"Seven."

"How did you get here?"

The question confused her. Did he mean how did she get here, like how Mommy explained about babies and pregnancy? Or did he simply mean how come she was in his house? "What do you mean?"

He laughed at her. "Who brought you here, Imani? Don't tell me you came all the way over here to lay on my pillows and listen to my music all by yourself? Not that I'd mind or anything, but someone had to bring you, right?"

"Oh. My aunt Lilly brought me." She lowered her voice. "You know Bryan's her boyfriend?"

He laughed again. "Yes, I knew that. Where did they go?"

"In the kitchen."

"Leaving you here all by yourself?"

"I don't mind. It almost like my house, but my house is prettier."

"Is that right?"

"Yes. Mommy makes women, so there're women everywhere looking at you."

"She makes women?"

"Uh-huh. Out of stone and wood and stuff."

"She's an artist?"

"I guess." Imani scooted closer to him until she was sitting directly across from him, hands folded in her lap. "Can I touch your hair?"

"You don't have any bad vibes or evil spirits lingering about you, do you?"

Imani slowly shook her head. "No. No, I don't think so. Someone would have told me by now, don't you think?"

He was smiling. "Yeah, probably. Go ahead, you can touch it."

Imani moved even closer until she was sitting surrounded by the waterfall that was his hair. His hair was black at the root and got lighter and lighter until it was almost blond toward the ends. She touched the ends first because they were nearest to her and moving in ripples and waves across the pillowed floor. It was hard but it wasn't hard. Stiff but beneath the stiffness there was this incredible softness that allowed Imani to shape and mold and part the thick mass of waves.

"Why is it so light down here?" she asked.

"The older the locks get the more exposure they get to the sun. The sun did that, made it lighter, bleached it."

"I thought that the sun made things darker."

"I guess it depends on what kind of things you're talking about. See, the sun makes people darker, right? But it makes other things like hair lighter. You get me?"

"Yes." She moved even closer. He smelled like outdoors, like trees and grass and sun; it was a good smell. She ran her hands up the length of his locks, starting from the blond puddle on the floor and working upward until she was touching the midnight darkness of his roots, a darkness that melded and blended into his skin. She pulled away from him, settled on her knees in front of him.

"How does it feel?" he asked.

"I think that you have the prettiest hair that I've ever seen. I think that you are the prettiest person, besides Mommy."

"Well, I thank you. Aren't you quite the heartbreaker."

She gazed at him. "I don't break hearts."

"No, I don't imagine you do quite yet. But give it time."

Aunt Lilly and Bryan came back into the room and Imani's smile faltered. Aunt Lilly was stumbling a bit and holding on to Bryan and Bryan was holding on to her like he would fall flat on his face if he let her go. Aunt Lilly tripped over a pillow and went stumbling down hard.

"Aunt Lilly, you all right?"

"Sure I am, darling, darling mine."

Aunt Lilly's eyes were glassy and wet and so wide that they seemed to be staring into eternity. She couldn't keep her mouth closed, it was open and red and vulnerable. Aunt Lilly swayed and tilted and finally Bryan pulled her down next to him and they sprawled out on the pillows, eyes closed, breathing so heavy that it could be heard over the music of men leaving and lying and cheating.

Imani looked up at Taji. He was perfectly still and so tense and he said, "I can't believe you all did this. You brought a child here and did this?" He was angry and all of a sudden Imani was scared.

"Aunt Lilly?" Imani's voice was trembling. She wanted Mommy. She wanted to go home. She wanted Mommy's arms and the red heart of Mommy's room.

Taji bent down to her and lifted her. "Come here, baby. It's okay. It's okay."

Imani shook her head and the tears came, little-girl tears all at once. "What's wrong with Aunt Lilly? How come she won't get up?"

Taji rubbed her back, smiled at her. "She just tired, Imani. That's all. Her and Bryan both are just tired. How about we go outside on the steps?"

"What about Aunt Lilly?"

"She'll be all right. I'm going to take you outside."

Outside was sun and heat and children shouting and running and men and women laughing and talking, not like the darkness and coolness of the house, the absolute still-ness of Aunt Lilly and Bryan lying upon the hardwood floor. Imani allowed Taji to place her in his lap. He was big but not man-big and smelled good and some of her fear left her.

Imani buried her face in his shoulder, his hair, and he held on to her, rubbing her back, making clucking noises with his tongue the way that Mommy sometimes did when Imani ran to her bed after a bad dream. She wondered what in the world was wrong with Aunt Lilly. Was she sick? Did she get one of those headaches that she was always getting, headaches that knocked her off her feet and forced her to lay down with the television real, real low until the pain passed? Was Bryan sick, too?

She took a deep breath and raised her head, fingers playing with the blond ends of Taji's hair like he was Mommy even though she knew he wasn't. "Aunt Lilly going to be all right?"

He was staring at her, eyes wide and helpless and deep, deep brown. "She'll be okay. She just needs to lay down for a while."

"Why you angry with her? She and Bryan do something bad?" She was watching him because there was something that he wasn't saying, something that everyone wasn't saying but thinking, all the time thinking about Aunt Lilly.

"She shouldn't have brought you here. She should have had more sense, knowing what Bryan's into and what he's dragging her into."

"Oh," Imani said and none of it made any sense to her. The black and green and red door of the house was directly behind her and she stared at it, thinking about Africa and people who looked like her. Aunt Lilly said that Bryan was a panther, like the big cat in the jungle, but he didn't eat animals or people or small lost children. He was a fighter, a fighter who fought for all the black and red and yellow and gold people. How could he fight when he was sprawled out on the floor, not moving or speaking, the whites of his eyes red and blurred and burning?

They sat on the stoop, Taji waving to people he knew

and talking to women who watched him with thoughtful, coveting eyes. Beautiful women who were round and brown and black or slim and yellow and red. Women with short hair and hair that fell down their backs and hair in braids and large halolike Afros. Women who seemed happy and weightless and carefree and women who smiled so sadlike and looked as if they were holding the weight of the world upon their shoulders, as if at any minute they would snap and break and the world would fall all to pieces. Imani sat close to Taji and the women asked her questions and wondered who claimed her and touched her hair and forehead, the slender curve of her neck.

The women came and went until they were all gone. It was dark and getting cool, and Imani shivered.

"You cold?" Taji asked, pulling her closer into his body.

Imani nodded. "I want to go home." She was tired now, the shock and worry of seeing Aunt Lilly sprawled out and dazed catching up with her.

Taji just watched her and then sighed so deep, like it was coming from way down inside of him and he was reluctant to let it out. "Let's go see how Lilly's doing."

Just the mention of Aunt Lilly's name brought the anger back in his voice, and Imani wanted to ask him why but she was scared of what he might say, scared to hear what everyone was thinking and no one saying about Aunt Lilly.

The house was dark, no lights on, and silent, the music of men lying and cheating and leaving faded and gone. Taji turned on a light. Aunt Lilly and Bryan were still spread across the floor and pillows. Taji went over to Aunt Lilly and shook her.

Aunt Lilly opened her eyes and closed her mouth. Taji was standing over her. "What . . . ?" she asked and then she sat up quickly, nervously. "Oh, God. Imani?"

"Don't act like you give a damn now."

"Imani?" Aunt Lilly asked again, eyes wide. Bryan was snoring next to her; he rolled into her and wrapped his arm about her waist. "Get off of me. Imani?"

"I'm okay, Aunt Lilly." Imani wanted to go to her but she didn't know Aunt Lilly this way and she moved away until her back was hitting the door.

Aunt Lilly crawled over to her; Imani watched and tried not to cry. "Hey, baby, darling mine. You okay? Tell me you okay?"

Imani shook her head. "I want . . . I want to go home."

Taji dragged Aunt Lilly to her feet. "Stop it. Look at her face, you're terrifying her."

"I'm sorry. I'm so sorry."

Taji just stared at her, distant and cold and mean. "Yeah, you are sorry."

Aunt Lilly pulled away from him, her eyes glaring and her mouth harsh. "You don't know shit."

Aunt Lilly was hard and brittle and Imani wondered if she would break, or if she would hurt Taji, go for his throat like a panther, even though panthers weren't suppose to eat people. "Aunt Lilly, I want to go home." She was crying, quiet tears.

Taji said, "Lilly, I'm going to walk you home. You ready?"

Bryan was still sleeping on the floor. Aunt Lilly said,

"Baby, I'm leaving now. I'll see you soon." He didn't answer her, just kept snoring. Aunt Lilly kissed him.

"Girl, what's wrong with you?" Taji asked.

"Like I said before. You don't know nothing about it."

"I hope to God I never will. I tell you this much, this is my house. Bryan will be out on the streets tomorrow. You go and meet him there."

They left Taji's house, Imani walking between them. Aunt Lilly and Taji didn't say two words. Grandma and Mommy were sitting on the stoop in front of Grandma's house. Imani broke free of Aunt Lilly and ran to Mommy and was held as if she were gone for weeks not a half day. Mommy said, "I was so worried. I came back from New York and Mama didn't know where you all were and I was so scared. Look at me. Let me see your face." It was dark out but Mommy noticed the mess of her tears. "You've been crying? Lilly, where did you take her? And who is that?"

Grandma was small and dark and her face was round and thin. "Lilly, where have you been? Look how late it is. Don't you have any sense?"

"Who are you?" Mommy asked Taji.

"I'm Taji. Lilly was visiting her boyfriend, Bryan, who used to stay with me. I walked her and Imani home. You have a beautiful child."

Mommy spun fast on Aunt Lilly, noticing her bleeding eyes and the way that she seemed light and clumsy on her feet. "Say something. Tell me not to think what I'm thinking. Tell me, Lilly. Tell me you love my child too much to have her around something like that."

Aunt Lilly was quiet for a long time and then she said, "Rose, I'm sorry. You know I didn't mean . . ."

Mommy just stared at Aunt Lilly, then her head fell and her voice came out soft. "Oh, Lilly, darling mine, sorry isn't good enough."

Studio Time

AIR IN HER STUDIO smelling like all the good smells of her house and Rose having difficulty breathing it in, air made thick and heavy and she was thinking about Lilly and Lilly dazed and sitting in Mama's living room and Imani sitting quiet and still on her lap the last time that they went to visit. Fresh bruises lining her arms and Lilly holding Imani, leading Imani like she had good sense and wasn't fucked up out of her head.

Rose's hands on hard wood, feeling for the texture beneath the hardness of brown flesh. Hands moving fast and furious and in her head the image of Lilly zoning out in her room or bathroom or alleyway or some man's house, and wood beneath her hands taking on the fragileness and unfocused hardness of some woman drugged up out of her mind. Lilly happy to get high and watching her fade in and out like bad reception on some old black-and-white television and nothing she could say or do about it because Lilly doing exactly what Lilly wanted to do.

First time she realized that there was nothing going to make Lilly who she was before she started running the streets with belts tied around her arms and needles like jewelry piercing her flesh was when Lilly brought Imani home over a year ago with Taji. Watching them walk toward her and anger and disgust humming off of Taji and sadness and tears from her child and looking into Lilly's face and it was so obvious that she was coming down from a high, eyes blurred, head light and fluid and too heavy for her body. Rose knew Lilly loved Imani, loved Imani almost like she was hers—and shooting up more important than Imani and Imani's safety.

Only thing she wanted to do was hurt Lilly like Lilly had hurt her, hurt Imani and Mama and Violet, hurt anybody tied to her by blood and flesh and history. Imani and Lilly crying, crying together like they were both little girls. Hearing Imani crying over a woman who loved belt tied around flesh and needle piercing skin more than she loved her or anything and anyone else.

Imani heavy and leaning into her side, wanting to be picked up and she couldn't, she just couldn't move her body to make herself bend down and lift a seven-year-old child. Lilly watching her, wet tears, wounded and sorry, so absolutely sorry. Some strange man was holding Lilly up and staring at her like he had seen her before, like they were old friends who had simply lost contact and the first time that she really looked at him found herself wondering over his wide, wet, woman's eyes.

Taji's wide, wet, woman's eyes so different from eyes of black men talking black culture and black politics, men in and out of her and Imani's life, in and out of her house and bed. She knew that long wrap skirts and dashikis and head wraps and one or two more black faces in Congress or the Senate or mayor of some predominantly black city somewhere wasn't enough to make everything in her life and the lives of her mama and her sisters and other black women with no babies or babies and more babies tugging on skirts, good jobs or no jobs at all, good husbands or no husbands, better.

Black men with eyes glazed over and emotion turned down or off or maybe just hidden because men weren't supposed to show emotion and the only thing they had to offer her was limited kindness and politics, but still better than guilt always eating at her when she thought about how she failed to be a part of Black Liberation in the beginning, how she turned her back, went somewhere she was never supposed to have gone. No glaze over Taji's eyes and staring at him and wondering what was there, what he had that no one else seemed to have and something inside her shifting and moving toward him.

Staring and wondering about him and a great, wide hole opening in front of her and falling into it, falling headlong into the past and that place that she never was supposed to be. Charles and the moistness of his breath against her and the softness of his skin and the way that his eyes were always wandering, never quite focused. Sitting up with Charles night after night in the apartment on South Street, listening to people walk up and down the sidewalks between Fifteenth and Second and South like all they had to do was keep walking and eventually find beer or wine or hard liquor or weed or heroin or speed or coke or a warm, willing body. Keep walking and everything they ever needed or dreamed of needing right there behind dark doorways, under bright lights of clubs, alleys and a little light from street lamps filtering in. Charles talking to her about being young and the suburbs and Main Line and happy and not really coming into the city at all unless it was to buy drugs or liquor or hang out at one of the peep shows on Market Street. Not until he saw all those people on television being beaten with nightsticks and held off with dogs and water hoses and carried away in handcuffs, most of them younger than him, did he start thinking about how privileged he was and what that privilege meant and who that privilege damaged. His privilege was part of the reason why children were being beaten down by water hoses and chased down by dogs and carried off to jail.

He left the suburbs and Main Line as soon as he was able, as soon as he was old enough that whatever anyone said didn't make the slightest bit of difference, and besides, he wanted to write and the suburbs and Main Line didn't understand why he didn't want to go out and make something out of himself, especially since he had been given so much.

Night after night and he told her that he was a different person, that who he had been he didn't really like, had never liked. It took the year on South Street for both of them to realize that who he was was in his blood and bone.

Taji

THERE WAS SOMETHING about the scent of a woman, the body and breath and purpose of a woman that Taji was always looking for with gold red blue black almost white women and women with braided hair down the back or swinging straight or fluffed high or scalps clean shaven and bald. Scent of a woman constantly moving inside him, moving like rivers, like air long before puberty and first wet dreams and all the time thinking about skin against skin.

He fed at Mama's breast, had a sister almost six years younger than him and always cleaning up after her, wiping dirt and nastiness from brown plump flesh, letting her sleep with him at night when bad dreams had her scared to turn off lights or go to the bathroom all by herself. Mama and his sister, Sandy, and sharing a house and dreams and future with both of them and it never occurred to him that out there in the world there were men who didn't like women, didn't need women except to fuck or hurt. Men out there who weren't constantly looking for the scent of a woman because it was good and home and Mama's milk and skin moving against skin.

At his desk in his small house and his desk was placed in the master bedroom upstairs, space with the most windows and the most light and trying to do a write-up for the radio station about community spirit or the waxing and waning of community spirit. He was a journalist for one of the only black radio stations in Philly, one of the only stations that catered to the black community and really cared about the things—political policy, crime, drugs, housing, public schools, voting—that the black community was always struggling with and always trying to get a handle on. Trying to get at new ways for people stunned by everything that went wrong in the last five or so years to get involved again and thinking about the scent of this new woman that was always with him. This new woman, Rose, and he knew nothing about where she came from or where she'd been, all he knew was that she had a child, Imani.

His room dim because only the table light was on and walls painted muted shades of brick red and white carpet soft and plush under his feet. Outside the sun going down and children running up and down the small driveway, small spaces between houses, and from his window they were blurs in bright-colored jackets and frantically waving arms and kicking feet. The scent of this new woman all in his head and the scent more important than the prettiness of her face or body, more important than arms that held tight or arms that pushed away. The scent of her like dark earth, like damp earth, red clay and her skin was red and golden and brown, so many colors like soil was so many colors, a different color at each layer.

Thinking about the past five years or so and everything that went wrong that could possibly go wrong and entire communities falling apart after all that talk about equal rights and moving forward and the irony of it all eating at him. Only a few who lived where he lived and looked how he looked and talked how he talked moved forward. The rest no better off than they were before the whole thing started and everyone caught up in Civil Rights and Black Power and change. He missed a lot of it, especially in the early sixties because he was in New York and everything that was happening down South seemed far away even though he sat faithfully in front of the television for the evening news each night like everyone else. Watching black people get heads, faces, bodies bashed in and white people looking self-righteous and confused and angry. Everyone angry and he was waiting, like every black person under the age of thirty, for black people to get sick and tired and fight back.

He guessed that's why the government recruited so many young black men for the Vietnam War, better to have them in Vietnam killing brown and yellow people than in the heat and swamps and long days and lush green of the South or the concrete and steel and people living on top of each other without any room to move, to step outside and breathe air not already used ten times over by millions of people in the North. Vietnam making brothers crazy and he was thankful that he went during the tail end of the war,

stayed for a year and then the war was over, lost, and they
sent everyone home.

Before he left for Vietnam watching Black Panthers on
television and being impressed with guns and arrogance and
no fear, Black Panthers standing up to cops and patrolling
streets with weapons ready. Black men willing to stand up
and be men and he knew that that was what Black Power,
Black Liberation was all about. The unapologetic maleness
of the Black Panther Party, of Black Liberation seducing
him into forgetting his mama and sister's scents, the scent of
a woman that was always in his head, like music. He
scrubbed the scent off with a rough scouring pad until his
skin was raw and when he thought of women there was
nothing there but pretty faces and firm breasts and nice,
round asses.

Black Panther Party taking on United States of America
and fighting in a way that America had never seen black
men, black people fight before. Taji loved the empower-
ment, loved black needs and black community and black
economic and political agenda coming first and no room to
compromise because look where compromise had gotten
them up until this point. Taji and his comrades walking
through the streets of New York, policing neighborhoods,
policing the police, running a free breakfast program for
children in their neighborhoods, making a difference and
they were bad motherfuckers.

There were no women. They were there in the background and every now and then there was the whisper of
their voices at some meeting or other, whisper because talk
too loud and they were silenced by what black men needed

to do and how black men needed to get together before they could start thinking about sisters. Wasn't really an issue because everyone knew that sisters had it easy all along, sisters working when black men couldn't find jobs, sisters sleeping with white men and getting over while black men wasted entire years of their lives on street corners, tuned out and off on drugs and no one there to help them out or pull them up because sisters too busy doing for sisters and always quick to say a black man ain't shit and no one else gave two fucks either way.

Taji sitting at his desk and trying to write a piece about black people getting involved in their community again and the children outside his window, running back and forth through the small drive, in and out of the small spaces between houses and their laughter like something a bit too loud and almost obscene and it was almost dark and time for mamas to start calling children in. When he was young his mama called him in as soon as the sun faded a bit in the sky; now mothers were young and the children were out running early in the morning and late in the evening and the children were almost raising themselves because no one was around to tell them what they should and shouldn't do.

Pen and paper like ball and chain in front of him, paper sprawled all over the deep dark wood of his desk and he was all the time wondering how to go back, to take everyone who looked like him and talked like him and lived where he lived back. Back and stand still in that time that was gone, that they lost, and try to learn what they failed to learn the first time around and he had no idea of what that was. Then again, there was always moving forward, and that's what most people were trying to do and making a mess of it all, tripping over feet, getting tangled up in wants and needs and disappointments and falling on faces frozen permanently with shock and something like despair eating at the heart.

Taji twirling the pen aimlessly in his hand and staring blankly at the paper and thinking about the Black Panther Party and Black Liberation and women rarely seen or heard, just fucked, and thinking that maybe it couldn't have turned out any other way.

Thinking back and just about every brother he knew lived with a woman. One of his best friends then, Quincy, lived in Brooklyn with this girl that he had been seeing for maybe a year. Her name was Natasha and she was beautiful the way that sisters involved with Black Liberation were supposed to be beautiful. No permed hair but intricate braids with multiple beads swinging at the tail of each, no makeup but skin glowing and healthy the way that skin looks when women have little else to think about and little else to do than give themselves facials with the flesh of avocados or sit at the kitchen table and prepare oatmeal face scrubs. Natasha, this beautiful woman, playing a part for Quincy scripted by the demands and confines of Black Liberation.

He was all the time over their house then, and all the time watching them interact and trying to figure out what about them and their situation and his situation didn't ring true, what about the whole thing had Natasha so scared and so nervous and always biting her nails or pulling absently at the tails of her braids. Coming into the door of their house and immediately confronted with posters of black people on the wall and paintings by black people all throughout the house and Coltrane or Muddy Waters pushing at the air and the smell of something good, something spicy and almost Southern coming from the kitchen, and incense burning and standing in the middle of the space she created was Natasha waiting for some kind of praise or approval and biting anxiously at her lower lip.

Quincy, small dark brother with full lips and huge hair, came through the door without kisses or anything that resembled some kind of greeting between lovers, between kings and queens. First thing out of his mouth usually something like, "What the hell is that smell? What you cooking? Shit, woman, why is it so dark in here? What have you done with yourself all day? See what I mean, Taji, brother out all day fighting the good fight and coming home and ain't nothing in order, ain't nothing the way it's supposed to be."

Natasha moving about the apartment, trying hard to fix whatever Quincy said needed fixing and getting food and getting drinks and pens and paper so that they could sit on the couch or sprawl out on the floor and brainstorm about all the things that black people needed, all the things that black people weren't getting. Natasha the whole time rushing back and forth between them, braided beaded hair flying and chewing on her lower lip and fingernails bitten almost bloody. Natasha never stopped moving and they never stopped to ask her what she thought or what she felt or did she have any ideas maybe about the best way to proceed on any issue.

Natasha was like something caged and dependent and he

was all the time watching her and trying to figure out why watching her and her anxious, nervous movements made him feel so bad. Bad like he felt when he was in grade school and watched younger, smaller boys being teased and hit on the playground. Bad like he felt in Vietnam when he just walked away from starving women and children, when bullets from his gun tore through the insubstantial doors and windows of village houses, tore through skin and flesh and blood because there was no telling where the Vietcong were hiding, no telling who they were and the commanding officer always telling his platoon that they all looked alike anyhow and what difference did it make.

Watching Natasha and watching Natasha and all the blue black red gold brown women living with brothers and keeping house and raising babies because there were no other options and a tension eating at the healthy glow of their well-tended skin, making their thick and lush hair thin and fall out at the roots, and eyes either constantly moving looking for a way out or absolutely still and looking inward, gone to the rest of the world. After days, weeks, months spent watching and the Black Panther Party in trouble and falling apart all around him he noticed that these women had no scents. They had perfume, perfume slathered on and making a room smell like them as soon as they walked in and long after they left. They had incense, incense always burning and house always blurred with incense smoke.

But no scents, not the way that his mama and sister and all the women that he dreamed and wondered and worried about and touched and held before he left for Vietnam.

Scent getting at the heart of a woman and telling him everything important that he needed to know. Scent overwhelming strong and seductive and no need at all to look at and consider prettiness or lack of prettiness, big ass or no ass at all, nice breasts or breasts that hung, slender or wide hips.

Taji sitting at his desk and trying to write an article abut black people getting involved again and aimlessly pushing his pen across blank paper and thinking about the scent of a woman, that scent that he was always looking for beneath heavy or light perfume, beneath coconut or sickly sweet hair oil. He wanted to be surrounded by a woman's scent again.

Rose's scent constantly in his head, woman that he couldn't help following through streets and alleyways because her scent that overpowering, pulling him to her.

Studio Time

H E WAS FOLLOWING HER, Rose knew it and knew that she should be scared, at the very least annoyed, but instead she was charmed. Charmed to leave her house and see his smiling dark face, charmed to look behind her and watch as he swept his hair, the long, thick length of it, behind his shoulders, away from his neck and eyes; charmed by the sight of his slim, muscular body, lean and tall and elegant, not stocky and broad and intimidating, the way that men could be sometimes. She wondered why he didn't speak, didn't acknowledge her really except for the occasional smile or brief meeting of eyes.

Rose stood at her sink washing dishes and thought about his watchful and careful presence in her life. It was late morning and Imani was at school and dishes from last night's dinner piled in the sink and Rose standing there in robe and barefoot thinking about Taji.

Sometimes Taji came over to bring Imani fresh plantains and coconut milk, stood in Rose's house talking to her child, occasionally smiling at her, saying no more than he had to, and enjoying Imani's company so much that how could she have told him not to come around? Imani's smile wide and open, staring up at him, her eyes following him so hard and so carefully, her hand constantly in his, her arms sneaking around his neck and holding tight to the warmth and the skin beneath the wave of hair. Taji's laughter rising up in the still air of afternoon and making the wooden or stone faces of her women smile.

Rose didn't say much, just sat and watched them and wondered if Imani really missed a man's presence. Rose didn't mind having women shape and define her existence. Women were soft and round and smelled like kitchens and food or like subtle musk, sometimes too-sweet perfume. Mystery and magic hidden behind the ears, between the breasts, behind the back of the knees, and silk of the inner thighs. The men in and out of her life stayed a little while, never forever, but women were for all time, like Mama, like Lilly and Violet, like Imani and the women she sculpted.

Rose knew that Imani was waiting, constantly waiting for an explanation or a name or the description of a face or the sound of laughter or the strength of hands or the length of hair or the complexion of skin. Imani was the only proof that she had that she was ever kissed and held and touched and fucked by a man whom she lived with for a year when she was eighteen. And the guilt, the guilt over where she had been making it impossible to hold on to memories, easier to just let everything fade and start all over—new self and new lovers and new decisions and no reason to go back and ever be that girl that she was again.

The dishes were done, stacked and left to dry on the side of the sink. Rose went to the refrigerator, retrieved apples and oranges and pears, went to the kitchen table and began cutting and slicing fruit for her breakfast. At first she thought that Imani simply liked the company of men, like some children do, and that was why being around men and men's ways caused her to smile quick and watch with complete attentiveness as they walked across hardwood floors and scattered themselves among throw pillows and talked with deep, rumbling man voices.

Rose knew her father, loved her father, never looked in the faces of other men hoping to see hints of her father there or hoping to create a father from scratch, from imagination and dream space, like Imani did.

She had tried to create space where there was none with Imani's father, tried to shift and manipulate and carve out her insides, all on someone else's terms, and it didn't work. Her heart, back then, didn't beat in healthy rhythms, it beat in spasms, clenched and angry, and sometimes she thought that the spasms would kill her, leave her open and the bright red of her blood exposed and no one around to mop it up or help her put herself back together again.

It was the pregnancy and the fear of falling apart for good, falling apart and wandering the streets, which weren't nice or safe or clean, that forced her to leave. The leaving was hard, all the arguments and tears and his fists striking walls and his hands throwing furniture, or roughly or tenderly cradling her face, or shaking her so hard that she couldn't think, literally couldn't form a thought and just wanted to sit down somewhere and have a good cry or take a knife to him when he fell asleep. He was in mortal danger and just too stupid and blind to realize it. She would have killed him, thought about it the first time he let the word "cunt" drift from his lips while kissing her, the first time he asked "my pussy?" while inside of her.

She was damn near crazy, leaving the first time, and she promised herself that no man, nobody would ever force her to leave anywhere, especially her own home, again. So simple, to cut some emotions, to hide others, to love daughter and family and nothing else, to have pleasant sex with pleasant men and send them on their way.

The fruit was cut into neat, precise slices and Rose put it all in a large bowl, added yogurt and sprinkled a little honey in it. Fresh fruit in the fall or winter always made her smile, it was so unexpected to walk into a supermarket and see everything ripe and bleeding with color along the produce aisles. She liked simple meals, fresh fruit and vegetables, brown rice and beans, occasionally fish.

Taji wasn't a stranger, she knew him, knew his laugh and his smell and his voice. When he left after visiting Imani his scent would be all through the house, frankincense and something else, something that was absolutely and completely his. She spent nights alone in bed thinking about that scent, wondering over that scent, her hands roaming her body and imagining what he would taste like. All that dark, smooth skin laid out before her and underneath her, that elegant man's body, and his wide woman's eyes watching her as she did all sorts of things to him and allowed him do all sorts of things to her, unspeakable acts to give unspeakable pleasure.

She wanted to touch him, spent long hours contemplating just where and how, but she also wanted to talk to him. Talk to him the way that she stopped to talk with the black and brown and red and yellow men at the stoop on the corner, working at their own businesses in the neighborhood, walking their kids to school, on the way to pick up their wife or daughter or mother. She wanted to watch the words fall from his mouth, watch the words linger on the tongue and hover at the corner of the lips before rising into the air precise and beautiful and offering her a place in his world, even if it was just a small place, even if it was just a place carved out in passing.

Phone Conversation

"MAMA?"

"Hey, why you calling this early?"

"I don't know. I thought you'd be awake. You know you get up at the crack of dawn."

"That don't mean that I'm just sitting around waiting for you to call."

"No, it doesn't. I just wanted to talk to you and right now the boys and Jerome are asleep . . . I don't know, Mama."

"Don't know what?"

"I've been wrapped up in Jerome and this us and this life that we were trying to have and this family that we were trying to build for so long . . . Everything is a mess and I know I'm staying with a man who doesn't love me anymore."

"You know, I never worried really worried about you. Not with Lilly and Rose running wild and demanding so much of my attention. You were always steady."

"That's the thing, Mama. I don't feel steady no more. I made this decision to marry this man and I believed in ever after, not necessarily happy ever after, but I never even imagined this. And Jerome just walks around like all is good."

"I've always wondered how some men can keep doing wrong no matter who they have to lie to or convince that they're crazy."

"I'm not sure if it's as easy as that, Mama. I mean, this is not the first time he's . . . Did you know that? Rose and Lilly and everyone else knew so I figured you knew as well."

"Oh, baby, no, I didn't know that."

"I'm not saying that it happened all that often but sometimes he would come home with another woman on his mind, another woman's scent riding his skin. Come home and talk to me and touch me and I knew he was touching and talking to someone else. And he knew I knew, Mama. He knew I knew. Know what I did then?"

"No, baby, I don't know what you did then."

"I made myself as perfect as possible. He likes my hair long and permed straight then curled. I made sure I had weekly appointments to the hairdresser's. I know Rose is always talking about how vain I am and that's some of it but not all of it. He likes me to wear nice dresses or slacks with high heels. I wore them. He likes his dinner on the table every night by six. I made sure dinner was never late. He likes me to wear makeup and perfume. Mama, I wore lipstick and blush to bed for him. Had a horrible time getting makeup out of the sheets and bedspreads but I did it."

"How did you feel, Violet? How did you feel when you

were doing all those things, what did you call it? When you were making yourself as perfect as possible?"

"See Mama, that's what scares me now. I don't know if I was feeling at all. All I knew was that I had this man, this good man that supported me and my kids and was nice and didn't ever raise his voice or hands to me in my house and I wanted to keep him."

"Violet. I never knew. Out of all my girls you were the one I never could see taking anyone's mess for any reason."

"Mama, I never saw it as taking mess from him. Didn't even begin to think about it like that until now because being as perfect as possible isn't working anymore. I saw it as keeping something that I wanted. That's all."

"And now?"

"Oh, Mama . . . I'm hanging on by my fingernails. At any moment I could fall."

Studio Time

S HE WANTED TO DO A SCULPTURE of a woman in mourning, mourning for a mother, a child, a lover, a friend, a hero, a revolution, in mourning for something lost. She was struggling with the sketch because it was easier to draw a happy woman, a heartbroken woman, an in-love woman, a sad woman, than it was to draw a woman bent over and numb with grief. Grief private like the sexual insides of a woman, crease upon crease folded over, hiding the center until the gentle and warm touch.

She had grieved like that after her relationship with Charles ended. Grief-stricken and terrified and she didn't want anyone to guess the absolute mess and softness of her insides. Red insides, pulsing blood, but a heart that was weak and lungs that couldn't draw anything that even remotely resembled a deep breath. Grief knocked her off her feet and sent her home and there was nothing left to her, nothing left but the baby and the huge belly. She was almost dumbfounded and wondering all the time how did she let this happen and how was she going to fix it?

She was home and pregnant and huge and watching television with Mama and Lilly and Violet—Violet's boys running through the house like they were mad—when a news brief flashed and a white man with impeccable clothes and hair perfectly placed and a face that was green beneath his tan announced that Martin Luther King, Jr., had been shot and killed. He said it with no emotion, but his hands were clenched on the desk in front of him and his eyes were wild and red from wanting, needing to weep. Words falling and tumbling through the air in slow motion, words reaching the ears one at a time so that it took a moment to place one after the other, to form a coherent sentence. The man on the television was still talking, eyes rigid and his hands clenched and mouth trembling, giving endless details that couldn't make a dead heart pump blood again or dead lungs draw breath. Lilly sat on the very edge of the sofa, hands pressing into her temples like she wanted to squeeze her head open. Violet sat on the floor with her knees drawn to her chest, head resting upon her knees moving slowly back and forth in a gesture like denial but just tired.

Rose wanted to cry but what she was feeling wasn't meant for tears, wasn't meant for curling herself into a ball and letting it all be washed away. Kevin and Keith had stopped running wild about the house to sit on the floor next to Violet and asked their mama every few minutes, "Is he really dead? Are they sure?"

The first gunshot sounded in the distance, followed by

another and another in quick succession. She knew that people were streaming out of their houses into the street to walk off the shock and the grief, to walk into anger that was cool and pristine and could numb the millions of tiny fists hammering against the heart, slashing and bruising the strongest of muscles. People running through the streets enraged and vengeful and nowhere to direct it besides Mr. Charlie who owned the neighborhood market, Ms. Johnson who owned the dry cleaners, Mr. Moore who managed the neighborhood State Store. People who looked like all the other people in the neighborhood, people who had a little but were struggling like everyone else, not special people, not people who would ever dream of putting a gun to Dr. King's head.

Mama was sitting next to her so still, leaning into her, pushing her back into the lush comfort of the old sofa. She felt Mama's child's bones, the smooth skin of the arm and the little-girl weight, little-girl weight looking for someone to pick up and carry and kiss and make better. She remembered when she was a little girl and Daddy was still alive and Mama sitting in the same sofa rocking her as dusk approached and all the light faded from the living room and they were left in semidarkness and stillness. She loved Mama most of all during those times, loved the way that her skin smelled of soap and too-sweet drugstore perfume, loved the way her pressed hair floated around her shoulders, loved the softness of her skin, the deep black that she burrowed into and fed on. Sitting on Mama's lap in stillness and no light, taking little nibbles at the round flesh of the breast and ass, at the long length of slender fingers, at the warm curve of the neck, and the edges and corners of the lips, at the flat belly lined with stretch marks from her and her sisters. Being rocked in Mama's arms and swallowing her whole, Mama sitting quietly, the smile on her face saying that it was okay to feed, to take whatever was needed.

Now there was no intimate dark and stillness, just the explosion of gunshots and the shouts and screams as people walked off grief and into anger, and inside Lilly trying to squeeze everything out of her head, Violet trying to make herself believe that it couldn't be true, her nephews puzzled and confused, and Mama gnawing at her sides, licking at the tears that wouldn't fall, not quite yet. At first she had to remember South Street and Martin and Malcolm hanging from the walls while her lover lay over top of her and in her and around her and whispered, "Black cunt." She couldn't move, just lay still for him and let his words rush over her, rush over her leaving her small and dirty and shamed, arms hanging limply at her sides, lying beneath him thinking about love and what she thought was love and wondering how she was going to get herself out of such a mess. Wondered how even as he kept whispering to help her understand that they were nothing but words, didn't have the power to hurt her even as she lay open, her insides red and shining at his feet. He didn't pick them up, didn't tenderly bend down and cradle the intestines, the kidney, didn't try to correct or understand the harm that he had done.

Dr. King dead and "black cunt" constantly in her ex-lover's mouth, and Mama feeding on her like she was a child, and Lilly trying to break open her head, and Violet and the kids wanting to play a game of make-believe, and she was sitting almost nine months' pregnant on her mama's sofa while outside guns were being fired and the neighborhood was being demolished by impotent hands. The tears came and she could not stop them.

Imani

AUNT VIOLET PROMISED HER that she could come over for the weekend and now Aunt Violet was trying to go back on her word. Aunt Violet didn't sound like she had a headache or fever or a cold or a bellyache, her voice was normal, and Imani didn't understand why she couldn't spend the weekend with her when her voice was normal. She called and called until Mommy said to stop calling and behaving like a spoiled brat and maybe Aunt Violet might feel better later on and come get her but later on was later on and it was raining outside and there was nothing to do because the door to Mommy's studio was closed and Imani knew better than to knock on it. Mommy just gave her this real distracted look and answered her without really talking to her and Imani knew that she was somewhere else.

Imani was hungry, the hunger rising up and making her stomach grumble. There was salad and black-eyed peas and homemade corn bread from dinner last night. Imani loved black-eyed peas, especially the way Mommy cooked them, letting them soak all night and then putting them on the stove and adding whatever it was she added so that the beans were soft and full of flavor and just a bowl full was enough to keep the stomach still.

Imani unfolded herself from the floor and went to the kitchen, hands playing in her hair, liking the feel of it undone and all over. It was soft and in some places matted and tangled and in some places falling smooth against the back of her neck and her cheek. The kitchen walls were yellow tiles and the curtains at the window white and the cabinets and cupboards green, green like grass or leaves before everything died.

She opened the refrigerator door and stood there, one hand in hair and the other on her hip and tried to figure out what she wanted. There was fruit, lots of fruit: apples and oranges and pears and grapes and even a few strawberries and cherries. There was bread, plenty of bread: fresh bread from the bakery near Grandma's and bread from the market and the corn bread that Mommy had made last night and all of it brown and smelling like butter and earth. There were vegetables, green and red and yellow and deep, deep purple. She took out the loaf of bread from the bakers near Grandma and sliced a big piece and put it in the toaster oven.

Imani pulled the toast out of the oven, scorching her fingers a bit and blowing frantically at first to cool off red skin and then slathering butter and honey on the bread. She ate standing, slowly circling the kitchen table.

The bread was done and the rain was easing, just a wetness on the ground and a dampness in the air that caused the windows to fog and sweat. Imani could hear Mommy coming down the steps and she tried to make herself look as miserable as possible. She sat at the kitchen table, placed her face in her hands, made her eyes huge, and let her lips pout. Mommy came into the kitchen, took one look at her face, and snorted with laughter.

"Look at you! I have never seen a child look more pathetic in my whole life. Is it that bad? Is life that awful?"

Imani tried not to smile. "Yes."

Mommy went to the refrigerator, pulled out some cherries and sat across from her at the kitchen table. "See, I made you smile. It couldn't be as horrible as all that."

Mommy was dusty and dirty, her hair tied up in a blue wrap and her overalls stained with all kinds of stuff.

"It's been raining all day."

Mommy sucked a cherry into her mouth and spit out the pit. "So it has."

"I can't go outside in the rain."

"You know, I think you're right, but it isn't raining now."

"But Mommy, look at the clouds. It could start raining at any moment. And what if I get dressed and go outside only to come back in when it starts raining again?"

Mommy sucked another cherry. "That's a possibility and imagine how awful it would be if you were in the middle of a game or something and all of a sudden it started raining and you actually got wet. I might have to rush you to the emergency room and remember how long we were in there the last time we went? Those people are awfully slow."

"See, now you making fun of me."

"I am, just a little. But what else am I supposed to do when I come downstairs and see you sitting at the table with your eyes stretched and your mouth drooping and you looking absolutely horrible and letting these heartfelt sighs come from deep inside and all of it because it's raining and you want to go outside?"

Mommy went to the trash and emptied the cherry pits and rinsed out her bowl. The phone rang and Mommy grabbed it off the wall.

"Hello? Hey, sister mine . . . Girl, you don't have to . . . You know that . . . She won't die . . . Okay. Okay. I'll see you in a few."

Imani was squirming in her chair. "Was that Aunt Violet?"

Mommy just stared at her and shook her head. "Yes, you wore her down. She's on her way to get you."

Imani leaped up and performed a little dance around the kitchen table. "Yeah, yeah, yeah! I'm going over Aunt Violet's, I'm going over Aunt Violet's . . ."

Mommy sat back at the kitchen table. "Imani, stop that. Stop that for a minute and listen to me."

Imani stopped dancing abruptly; just stood and stared at Mommy with big eyes because there was something serious in Mommy's voice and her face was smooth and firm. "Yes?"

"Imani, you shouldn't have bothered Aunt Violet like that. You made her feel guilty and now she's going to come and get you. Guilt isn't a nice thing to make anyone feel, especially when she told you, over and over again, that she didn't feel well."

"But when I talked to her she sounded fine, Mommy. Her

voice wasn't tight and soft and she wasn't coughing or anything and I just thought . . . I didn't mean to make her feel
guilty, really. I just wanted to go over her house."

Mommy stared long and hard at her. "Come here." Imani
climbed in her lap and clung, feeling miserable and awful, a
truly bad person. "My little girl. There are all kinds of ways
that people don't feel well. It's not just the body; often it's
the heart. It's Aunt Violet's heart that's hurting her and
when your heart hurts your voice doesn't crack and you
don't cough and you don't sneeze or have a fever or runny
nose. Your heart just weeps kinda softly inside."

Imani thought about that. "Is that what Aunt Violet's
heart is doing? Is it just weeping softly inside?"

"Yes."

"I didn't know."

Mommy tilted her face up to hers. "Listen, I want you to
be extra good and extra nice for Aunt Violet, okay? Try not
to give her any problems since she's nice enough to come
and get you."

Aunt Violet's car was brand-new and huge and bright
bright red and didn't make any sounds at all like Mommy's
car did. Uncle Jerome had bought it six months ago for
Aunt Violet's birthday. Imani was charmed at the idea of an
entire car for a birthday present. The seats were soft leather
and cream-colored, the inside of the car spotless because
Aunt Violet no longer had any babies and there was no one
around to dirty up her seats, leave handprints on the windows and stains from shoes on the carpet. The rain was
clearing up even though the sky was still gray and full and

round, like it had a big belly and had just eaten a huge meal. Imani kept switching her gaze from the window to the driver's seat because the clouds fascinated her, the way that they moved through the sky, lingered, and moved on, like a dance almost except that there was no music and no rhythm. Aunt Violet fascinated her, too, especially now that she knew that her heart was weeping softly. Imagine, a heart that didn't just pump blood and beat strongly in the chest, but cried.

Aunt Violet caught her staring and smiled. "So, baby, what are we going to do this weekend?"

Imani folded her hands in her lap and told herself how good she was going to be. "I don't know. I guess we can work on the quilt we started last time I was here if you feel up to it and all."

Aunt Violet laughed but her eyes were tired. "Of course, I do. That will be a lot of fun, actually. I haven't done any sewing in a while. I sort of miss it. And now I get to work on the quilt with my favorite person."

"Me? I'm your favorite person?"

Aunt Violet took one hand off the steering wheel and ran it over Imani's Afro puff at the crown of her head. "Oh, definitely. My absolute, best, favorite person."

Aunt Violet turned back to her driving and Imani just sat there, smiling to herself, smelling Aunt Violet's perfume that was like oranges and tangerines but not quite so strong and almost sweet and almost musk and the scented coconut oil that she put in her hair, and the mint that always lingered upon her breath. Mommy sometimes told Imani stories about how mean Aunt Violet was when they were all living in the same house and growing up and sometimes not quite able to stand one another let alone be civil. Aunt Violet had a temper, threw terrible tantrums that made Mommy look at her in fear and awe and Aunt Lilly burst into tears. She broke things, her own dolls, sometimes Mommy and Aunt Lilly's dolls and sulked and hid in her room when she didn't get her way. She beat up Mommy and Aunt Lilly if they breathed on her for more than two seconds and would have killed them just for looking in her direction. Imani couldn't see it, couldn't see this woman sitting next to her, so pretty and dark and graceful and smelling like all the good things that ever were being mean to anyone.

The sky opened suddenly and without warning and all the clouds ran into one another and there was just gray and water falling, falling and thudding against Aunt Violet's new bright bright red car. Imani watched, mouth opened, and wondered how anyone could see anything at all through the rain and the gray and there was absolutely no sun at all. Thunder raced through the skies and lightning parted the gray and Aunt Violet, as overwhelmed by it all as Imani, pulled to the side of the road.

Aunt Violet ducked her head and glanced out of the front window, sighed deeplike in her throat. "Okay. Let's just wait this one out for a little while. It looks like it should stop soon, too much force for it to go on for a really long time."

Imani moved closer until she was under Aunt Violet's arm, leaning against her side. "It's kinda pretty, isn't it?"

Aunt Violet glanced out of the driver's side window. "You think so?"

"Uh-huh. The way it kinda came down all at the same time. At first nothing at all and then all this."

"Yeah, I guess that's sort of impressive."

"And look, look how it changes everything. Like we in a storybook world and under a spell."

Aunt Violet laughed. "Yeah? Well, let's pretend we're in a storybook world. What would yours be like?"

"Me and you and Mommy and Aunt Lilly and Grandma would all live together in this giant house and there would be a forest with dragons and unicorns and some monsters, but they would be nice monsters. They'd only be mean if someone tried to hurt us. And there would be princes for all of you, and they'd be really cute and have all these horses that talked and told really funny jokes. And we'd be happy and have great balls and everyone would think that we're the most beautiful people in the world." Imani laughed. "I'm so silly! I forgot about Uncle Jerome. He can be your prince, you don't need a new one."

Aunt Violet's smile faltered, slipped, and righted itself. "I don't know about that. It seems to me that a woman can always use a new prince, particularly one who owns talking horses. Can you imagine that? What about you? No prince for you?"

"Nope. I'm too young for a prince. I have better things to do."

Aunt Violet grinned, delighted. "Yeah? Like what?"

Imani shrugged her shoulders. "You know, this and that."

"This and that what?"

"I figure someone's going to have to take care of all those

talking horses, right? That would be my main job, making sure that they had enough food and water and room to run around and someone to talk to. And then I'd have to go visit the unicorns and dragons and monsters in the forest to make sure that they were all right and spend some time with them so that they wouldn't think that I like the horses, as funny as they are, better than them. And the rest of the time I'd just play, play all day and all night and go to parties wearing a bright bright red dress like the color of your car."

"You're right. That sounds a lot better than being tied to some prince."

They were quiet for a moment and the rain continued to chatter fiercely about them. Imani asked, "What about you? If you lived in a storybook world what would it be like?"

Aunt Violet tightened the arm she'd sprawled over Imani's shoulder and pulled her closer into the warmth of her body. Imani closed her eyes and breathed her in, the almost sweet and almost musk scent that came out of a bottle and beneath it all simply Aunt Violet. "I don't know. Can't even think of where to begin, I've been living in this real world for so long. And in this real world there are no dragons or unicorns or nice monsters to watch over you. There's just you and the people you love and knowing that you can't protect them and hoping that they won't leave."

"Aunt Violet, I won't leave you, not ever."

"I'm almost selfish enough to wish that were true." She hesitated and then said, "Sometimes people leave for no reason. They leave you even though you see them every day and wake up to them every morning and they smile at you and try to convince you that they haven't really left."

Like the skies and the clouds that were hiding them in endless gray Aunt Violet began to cry and it was so deep and so powerful that Imani was transfixed and then utterly sad.

Studio Time

ROSE WAS DRAWING a rough sketch of a pretty woman, woman like Violet with big eyes and nice cheekbones and wide mouth and swinging hair. The woman's sketch coming along nicely beneath her fast-moving fingers and she watched the woman take shape and she was thinking about Violet, Violet like she was when she was a little girl.

Violet as a little girl always in dresses and ankle socks and shoes, hair always straightened and hanging down her back or up in a ponytail. Violet made Mama straighten her hair faithfully every Sunday before church. Sometimes Mama didn't have the time and Violet would rant and rave and stomp about and end it all on one long continuous sulk that could last for hours or days, depending on her mood. Mama straightened hair and ironed frilly little-girl dresses and kept white ankle socks white because she didn't feel like Violet's tantrums or attitudes and it was easier all around to just do what she wanted.

129

Rose and Lilly did what she wanted or stayed out of her way. Violet angry was like wind and ocean roaring and rain hammering down and nothing to do but wait it out because everyone knew that there was no way to stop it or get it under control. Yelling at Violet just made her eyes roll back in her head and all the muscles of her body tense. Beating her just made her more stubborn and more evil. Rose and Lilly all the time hiding behind doors and chairs or beneath beds and watching her in absolute fascination. Violet like no child they knew, like no child they had ever seen and they had to share a house and Mama and toys and television with her.

The sketch of the pretty woman was a little different than Violet's face, features a little more full, and not quite as much anger beneath the skin, leaving features pinched and small and skin dull and pale beneath the wash of color. Violet as a little girl raised hell whenever she felt like it, didn't care who saw her or who thought what or who was going to do what. Rose knew that it wasn't until Violet really saw the first boy watching her as she walked down the street, wasn't until the first boy licked his lips and winked at her and called her over to him with a voice sweet like anything Mama baked and breaking and sometimes high as her own and sometimes almost as deep as Daddy's voice was, that she started to swallow anger, choke on it, let it rot in her stomach. Anger rotting inside and Rose watched Violet talking to men and boys, eyes slyly innocent, voice and smile sweetly sour.

Violet sixteen years old and bringing Jerome home and helping Mama fix dinner and fetching him Cokes and making sure that he was comfortable and not raising her voice once, not even to laugh loud, and more makeup on than she usually wore because Jerome had told her that he liked his women done, and becoming whatever it was that he needed or wanted her to be. Rose knew that Mama watched, stunned quiet, because this girl-woman floating across the room in no way resembled her child.

Rose and Lilly didn't say much, just listened and tried not to get in anyone's way or do anything that might make Violet ugly and nasty later on because they just didn't have the energy to deal with that. They were cautious because Violet already told them that Jerome was the one she was going to marry. They knew, from hard and long experience, that whatever Violet wanted she usually got. Mama might have tried talking to her, probably something about starting out the way you meant to continue but Rose couldn't be sure and Violet was so hardheaded that she probably wouldn't have listened anyway.

Outside her studio window thunder screamed in the distance and Rose let charcoal fall from her hand and looked at the woman's face, big eyes and wide mouth and nice cheekbones, pretty woman. Pretty woman but sadness and meanness in the eyes and she thought that maybe all pretty women looked like that, had that same something ugly going on beneath the skin, burden of pretty too much and too heavy and women sad inside because they were scared to put the burden down.

Violet

THE DEEP HARDWOOD OF HER FLOORS bright from years and years of scrubbing and waxing and refinishing. The walls of the kitchen and living and dining and family rooms eggshell white, immaculate because her boys were almost grown and Jerome was never home. She spent her days in the house alone, cleaning, running errands, fixing her hair, playing with her makeup, trying on clothes. She felt like one of the dolls that she was always playing with when she was a little girl. One of the dolls that she carried around with her, and made clothes for, and sat on the dresser or the bed when she was tired of playing.

The middle of the night and her boys sleeping in the mess that was their rooms and she never went in there anymore, never told them what to do and what not to do because it wasn't like they listened to her anyway. Jerome was the head of the household and she was just wandering around and through rooms looking for something to do and trying to stay out of his way. Imani sleep upstairs in her bedroom, bedroom walls forest green and throw rugs thrown across hardwood floors and heavy cherry furniture, a man's room. Imani sleep in the king-size bed, buried beneath mounds of covers and sleeping the way that children sleep, curled into herself.

Violet wanted to go upstairs and lie down with her, wanted to fold herself around Imani's warm child body and breathe in her scent and let herself go. There was nothing like sleep for her anymore; at night she sprawled out on top of the covers of the bed and watched nighttime shadows play on the wall or counted the rhythm of her breath, the number of times that she blinked her eyes, or that her fingers and toes twitched.

She sat on the couch in the family room, old couch that smelled of the house and all of them. Smelled of the milk and juice that her boys drank all the time and spilled everywhere when they still boys, still hers. Smelled slightly of the dog that they had for a short time before she ran away, the rules of the house and when to shit and when to piss and when to eat a bit much for her. Smelled of first Christmases and all the Christmases since and the Old Spice cologne that Jerome had been wearing for as long as she'd known him. The cologne that the boys gave him faithfully each birthday and each Christmas, the cologne, since they were near to grown, that the boys had started slathering on before they went out the house.

Sipping at her tea made pale with milk and staring blankly at the television and the volume turned all the way down so that there were nothing but images and people trying to talk and open mouths that looked like pink and bloody wounds. Night air still outside and the thunderstorm earlier pounding away at garbage in the street and the sky deep black and no clouds, just a lonely moon.

Violet sipped her tea and tried not to think about who and what she was waiting on, tried not to think about him walking through the front door and his body fluid from recent orgasm and his mouth tender and soft about the edges and his smile lazy and his eyes full of pleasure and satisfaction that she had absolutely nothing to do with. That she hadn't had anything to do with for quite some time and she knew that they were just going through the motions and he liked it like that. Liked the fact that she allowed him to do whatever he wanted to do with whoever he wanted to do it with and her pleas and tantrums and threats didn't move him the slightest bit.

Her image of herself completely fucked up and distorted because she was not the kind of woman that waited up for a man, not the kind of woman that put up with some man's shit, not the kind of woman who just accepted and was grateful for whatever he chose to give to her. Lilly and Rose and Mama always talking about how mean she was and how much she liked having her way and she was sitting almost powerless in the family room that smelled of a family that she didn't know if she wanted, didn't know how to hold together much longer, and more tired than she had ever been.

And when he walked through the front door what was she going to say that hadn't been said, screamed, written down before? What other means or methods of communication open to her other than sticking a knife into his gut? The closest she ever came to actually hurting someone was ripping off the heads of Lilly and Rose's dolls, cutting off soft stuffed brown legs and arms, but she was all the time now thinking of hurting Jerome, thinking of hurting him and everything that she thought she wanted and all the ways that he had left her hurt and devastated without so much as taking the time to wonder about what she felt.

Her tea cooling and she topped it off from the porcelain teapot that Jerome had given her for Valentine's Day last year. He was always giving her things, like the new car that she really didn't want for her birthday this year because things were all that he had left for her and he could afford them and it demonstrated what a good husband he was to anyone who might be wondering why she was all the time looking so unhappy, looking like she had swallowed something bad and no way at all to bring it up.

She had married too young. Mama had tried to tell her but she didn't have time to listen to Mama, not with all her time spent running after Jerome and working at the Strawbridge's downtown as a perfume and makeup girl and making sure that Jerome had the financial and emotional support that he needed to finish his degree in public policy at the University of Pennsylvania.

She never had Rose and Lilly's love of something like writing or sculpting, something that she wanted to do more than anything else and something that was more important than anything else. She had Jerome and everything she had went to making him better than what he was. She learned to cook because he liked good food; Mama was amazed because cooking was something that she absolutely refused to do the entire time that she was growing up. After Jerome finished at the University of Pennsylvania and got a good job in city government, a job that practically guaranteed years of promotions and advancements, she taught herself how to give dinner parties, how many knives and forks and spoons and where each utensil went and the proper way to serve a meal. She went through stacks and piles of home-decorating books when they bought the house and each room in the house was done with colors and fabrics and textures that he liked and wanted.

Early sixties through the mid-seventies and watching the news and there were flames from one end of the country to the other, flames from North to South and East to West and she was young and in love and hardheaded and stubborn and foolish enough to think that none of it would have any kind of effect on her. She didn't live down South, she didn't live in any kind of Northern ghetto, she didn't live in housing projects, didn't need public assistance, didn't have a no-good man—she was safe.

She knew what Jerome could give her, what his promise to take her as wife meant. It meant house and cars and vacations once a year and no want. No hunger punching holes in her and her children's bellies, no fear of losing or not getting anything that she wanted, a roof over their heads, security. All those people out in the street fighting and picketing and marching over Civil Rights, and she knew vaguely that they were marching for her rights and that meant that she could live like everyone else, meant that the American Dream was there for them and right in their reach and neither she nor Jerome ever went to any kind of meeting or any kind of march or any kind of protest. They bought things, and more things, and had two boys and sent them to private school and never once felt even the beginnings of some kind of guilt.

Now she was all the time wondering: At what price things? At what price being pretty and keeping quiet? Fixing her hair hundreds of different styles and giving it one hundred brush strokes a night, having different shades of foundation and lipstick and blush and eye shadow for each season and happily ignoring the television and the news and radio and everything going on in her world because what her husband wanted and needed and what her kids wanted and needed and very rarely what she wanted and needed taking up all of her time.

She heard his car pull up in the driveway, the opening and closing of the driver-side door, his key in the lock and her entire body tense and a headache coming on. She was trying to get everything right and sorted out in her head, everything that she wanted to say and looking for a new way to say it all, a way that would force him to actually hear her.

Her tea cold and her fingers and hands clenched around the teacup and trembling slightly and tea made pale with milk moving like waves in the bottom of the cup, the tea bag a hard lump resting on her saucer. Sitting there on the couch in the living room and thinking about the first time she saw him and how young he was, how different he was from all the other boys and men that she had been dividing her attention between. Dividing her time between boys standing on the corner and boys driving around in stolen cars and boys heading off for college for the first time or coming home from college for Thanksgiving and Christmas break. Brown boys with shining skin and blue-black glowing boys and boys light yellow with red lips and cheeks and their color coming up when they got excited from rubbing against her or it grew cold outside. Boys with fast tongues and seamless, effortless rap and a way of walking that had her all the time following them with her eyes and womb. Jerome was skinny and shy and his face was still recovering from teenage acne and he walked like a white boy, all tight in the hips. But he was sweet and kind and she immediately saw the potential, saw the man that he would be five, ten years down the line and there was something sexually exciting, something that always left her wet and tingling when she thought about helping him become that man.

Jerome was in the house, she could hear his heavy, slow footsteps and the pause he made at the bottom of the stairs. She knew he was considering whether or not to go up to bed or come see about her in the family room, knew he was running through all of the possible unpleasant scenarios, knew he was thinking about all the other times that she waited up for him and what little good it had all done.

He was moving toward the family room, his footsteps slowing down and getting heavy like he had no idea why she was acting the way she was acting, why she insisted on making everything so hard for them, for herself.

Jerome rested against the arched entry to the family room, skinny boy with bad skin all gone and he was a man with almost grown sons, tall and slim and muscular and beautiful to look at. Always immaculately well-dressed no matter if he was going to the supermarket or the doctor's office or a child's birthday party. Right now his tie was loose about his collar, his shirt pulled carelessly from the waist of his pants, and his pants wrinkled.

"Hey." His voice was lazy and slow and patient like he used to be all the time with her before kids and house and mortgage and car notes, before she was changed forever with pregnancy and birth and taking care of Jerome and their kids the only options she had left.

"Hey." Waiting for him to say something else, and trying to ignore the cold tea in front of her, the hard clump of tea bag hanging from the rim of the saucer. No part of her body able to move and tears like pieces of flint lodged in her throat and chest. Her fingers and hands were clenched and ragged and dry like she was an old woman, her elbows pressing stiffly at her sides, her feet and legs swollen. Jerome a sickness in her house.

His dark eyes moving over her with something like puzzlement and something like pity. She knew what she looked like, knew what he saw. Woman sitting around waiting on a man looking half crazed, dirty silk nightgown hanging to ashy knees, ashy feet tucked and folded beneath the coffee table, nail polish chipped on fingernails bitten short and ragged. Her usually done and curled and styled for him hair all over her head and her scalp flaking and face bare, no makeup making lips fuller and cheeks higher and eyes bigger.

"Imani here?" he asked and she could just manage nodding, her head was that stiff on her shoulders. "I know she's sleeping in our bed, then. I'm just going to shower and crash in the guest room."

He was turning away, his back to her and just like that

she was dismissed and nothing left for her except the urge to plant something sharp and hard and long and deep into his flesh. Violet knew she couldn't let him go without some kind of resolution, some kind of anything that would make her feel better about herself and him and them. She pushed her stiff and tired body up from the couch and listened to the cracks and crying in her bones. "That's all, Jerome? That's it?"

He turned back to her and rubbed his hands over his face like he was trying to make her go away, leave him in peace. "I guess so, Violet. What else is there?"

Just that easy Violet was gone, pushed way past any point of handling him reasonably. "Motherfucker. Motherfucker . . ." Her voice was hoarse and ugly and not hers and he flinched like he was horrified at the filth coming from her mouth. "What else is there? Don't act like you don't know why I'm sitting down here . . . Don't act like you have no idea what's going on with me, what's going on with us." Violet was thinking about all the wasted time. Years of marriage and spending time the easy part, easy like putting on shoes and socks in the mornings, taking off all clothes and sliding beneath cool, clean covers at night. Violet thinking about time all around them and nothing to do, no reason not to waste and waste and try to find some ease in the middle of all that trash.

Jerome's hands running over his face again and a deep sigh coming from way down in his chest like he was trying to work with her and she was just making the whole thing impossible. "Violet, why we have to keep coming back to this? Look at yourself, look what you doing to yourself. And for what? I'm not going anywhere, I told you that."

Jerome was standing there well tended because she tended him and well fed because she fed him and successful because that's what she wanted and slaved over for him. Violet was all the time willing to be whatever he needed to keep family from going all to pieces, shattering to opposing ends of the Earth. "Fuck you, Jerome."

He turned away, footsteps heavy and slow, moving over well polished, shiny and bright hardwood floors. "I'm going to bed, Violet. See you in the morning." His steps became lighter and faster the farther he moved away from her.

Studio Time

G IRL CHILDREN WERE EASY and at the same time difficult to create. She often couldn't get past her own womanhood, couldn't rid herself of breasts and hips and ass and menstruating women's blood, couldn't remember her body and the way she felt in her body before the changes occurred. Changes that left the little girl she had been quiet and worried and cautious of her own flesh. Breasts instead of a smooth, flat chest and she couldn't run down her block, through her neighborhood, or the green of the park without feeling them rise and fall and rise even when she was wearing a bra. Breasts instead of smooth, flat chest and she couldn't run as fast, could barely keep up.

Rounded hips and ass instead of straight, girlish lines and her jeans didn't fit, couldn't be pulled over all that flesh. Woman's blood and every month there were cramps and she sat on the toilet seat holding her insides and watching her blood fall in large drops into pinkish waters.

She must have been looking forward to it, at least some

part of the girl that she was wanted breasts and hips and ass and blood. Some part of her wanted a woman's body and a woman's shape and a woman's heart. Growing up in the fifties and every image of woman just about everywhere white and made-up with pearls about the neck and hanging from the ears and she wanted to be like that because that was all she knew. She played in Mama's things, her perfume and clothes and makeup, girl child wandering about the house in high heels with fake pearls about the neck and smelling like too-sweet perfume with a painted-on slashing red mouth. She was charmed by herself, even though Mama would laugh and Violet and Lilly would tease and pile more makeup on her face until she looked like a little clown, her image totally distorted. She must have been practicing, practicing for breasts and hips and ass and blood and days when she absolutely wouldn't leave the house without eyeliner, blush, and lip gloss, wouldn't leave the house without smelling of scented oils and burning incense.

She must have been looking forward to it and then the change came, came roaring and a part of the girl she was silenced and kept still. Silenced in the face of her budding woman's vulnerability, silenced in the face of Mama's rules, silenced by what she could and couldn't do and how she should and shouldn't look. Girl child running free with abandon through the block, the neighborhood, the green of the park turned into woman walking slowly so that breasts will not bounce and hips and ass will not wiggle and wandering eyes will not follow.

Wandering men eyes traveling across and over and around her, wandering men eyes seeping beneath the skin and into the conscious and she saw herself through those eyes, saw the possibility of sex seared into her flesh, saw wandering eyes' fantasies that left her stripped naked and bare. Wandering eyes taking her outside of herself, so far outside of herself and so concerned with what she was or wasn't doing that she couldn't find the way back in, forgot even that there was an in until she had a girl child of her own.

Rainy, soft day outside of her studio window. Blue-gray skies and light fog in the distance, everything intimate and still. She sketched slowly, enjoying her work, listening to soft rain and the hush of a lazy day outside of her window. The soft rain had been falling for almost a week, soft rain that was like walking through mist and that would have been lovely if it wasn't so cold outside. Late fall and the heat turned up to eighty and leaving the house in heavy winter coats and scarves and hats and mittens. She was waiting for summer, started her silent vigil as soon as September rolled in and children were back in school and the days grew shorter.

Waiting for summer and waiting out winter and waiting for Taji always following her to speak. Taji with locked hair down his back and soft, wide, liquid woman's eyes and she wanted him. Wanted to feel smooth dark skin, dark like Mama's, and lean muscled body and soft or maybe rough locked hair. Taji following her with both body and eyes, trailing after her. But his eyes didn't take her outside of herself, didn't have her seeing the possibility of a new self through his gaze. An old trick that most men she knew had down pat, possibility of a new self, re-creation and reinvention and the name given to you by Mama or Daddy or somebody in the world who loves you completely forgotten. Name completely forgotten and nothing to do but love him hard because who else can you love?

Phone
Conversation

"MAMA?"

"Hey, Rose. How's Imani?"

"Violet came and got her. She's going to spend the weekend over there."

"How did Violet look to you?"

"I don't know . . . I guess bad, like she hasn't really been eating or sleeping and she's spending all her free time on something that she can't fix, not alone."

"I want her to come home. Told her that once, but I don't want to tell her again and have her thinking that I'm thinking that her marriage is over."

"Is that what you're thinking?"

"You know what? I'm thinking that she is unhappy and making herself ill over this man and she needs to come home. I don't care for how long and I don't care if she goes back. She needs to rest and be someplace where she knows that someone loves her."

"I feel so bad for her, Mama. No one ever tells you that

sometimes it just doesn't work no matter what you do or don't do or how badly you want it."

"Is that why you have men constantly coming and going?"

"Oh, Mama . . ."

"Wait, wait a minute. I wasn't criticizing, just asking a question."

"I don't know."

"Of course you do. I wondered after the whole thing with Charles was over how you would be the next time around. But you haven't allowed yourself to have a next time, you just have men coming and going and not a one of them is important to you. Is that easier?"

"Yes, it's easier because I'm not wrapping all of myself around this one person, not always shutting my eyes and shutting down my brain so that I can believe everything that he tells me, no matter if it's true or not, not always making myself believe that he is everything that I want and need until I can't remember what my own wants and needs are."

"Rose. Baby, you sound so angry."

"Not angry, Mama. Really. Just a little tired, that's all."

Rose

S HE OPENED THE DOOR and he was there, standing in
the downpour, the long length of his hair heavy and
weighted down and dripping, his clothes clinging to his
smooth dark skin and he looked smaller, no longer a man
but a little boy shivering and watching her with large, liquid
woman's eyes. The wet and damp had his scent drifting off
him in fragrant waves, like summers spent in gardens where
everything is pungent and fresh, and she was clenching her
thighs because his scent was so familiar, utterly his own, and
she dreamed about it, conjured him up in the middle of the
night, dark moonless night without reflection or apology
and secrets whispered into the hush, swallowed, never to be
repeated.

"Taji, what are you doing here?" she asked and he smiled
his slow hesitant smile and his words lingered at the corner
of his lips and smelled faintly of herbal tea and honey and,
dear Lord, she wasn't a vain woman but found herself taking
silent inventory of her appearance. She was coming from

her studio, so there was charcoal on her hands and jeans from sketching and probably some on her face. She was covered with little flecks of wood and stone dust and the scarf tied around her head was old and tired and her body was throbbing, just throbbing as if she had perfume behind her knees, between her breasts and thighs, chains of silver hanging from her ears, neck, and waist, and lavender scenting her breath.

"It wasn't raining like this when I left and all of a sudden . . . I went shopping earlier and I picked up some plantains and coconut milk for Imani and here I am wet and soaking and cold."

"I'm sorry, come in, please."

He closed the door behind him, stood there, dripping on hardwood floors, rain gathering and falling from the corners of his eyes. He sat his bags upon the floor and as he bent over the long graceful curve of his neck and back stretched and his hair spilled over his shoulder to graze the toes of his boots and he was so nicely put together, small and compact and strong and long-lashed tender eyes.

"You look like you're working. I don't want to bother you and I won't stay long. Is Imani around?"

"No. No, Violet came to pick her up yesterday, she's spending the weekend over there."

"Oh." And he ran his hands across his head, hair black and gold and smelling of rain and mist. "Oh, I'll leave this and just get out of your way."

"No, no, stay a minute. Come in and let me fix you some tea, get you a towel and some sweats and help you dry your hair." That was the most personal sentence that she had ever spoken to him; their talks consisted of her daughter, sometimes her work. She guided him up the steep and narrow stairs, leaving his bags filled with groceries for her daughter on the floor in the living room. She walked ahead of him and behind her could feel his heat and his scent was in front of her, leading her, seeping into her clothes and hair. She was amused and almost frantic with lust. She thought that only women possessed scents, were concerned with smells, knew that a scent lingered long after names, breath, and memory. The quickest way to seduce a man into leaving was to change the scent; wearing vanilla instead of musk or jasmine instead of patchouli hinted at unfamiliarity, no longer the woman, lover, friend that you once were and complex enough so that for some men staying made little sense.

The upstairs of her house was cramped and crowded, Imani's dolls banished from her room and leaning against walls or the torsos or heads or backs of women, stone and wood women, and a throw rug laid out across the hallway to keep the chill of late autumn and early winter from seeping unsuspectingly into the bones. Her bathroom was blue, like Mama's, with plants hanging from the ceiling and lining the windowsill and lilac curtains hanging from the windows and a lilac rug, clean and smelling of wind and earth because she hung it outside to dry, in front of the bathtub. It was a small corner of the house, cozy and warm and she spent hours in the tub, bubbles and fragrant waters up to her eyeballs and slender arms drifting over the side of the tub or holding a book and candles softly and surely burning. They were almost touching because there was nowhere to go, no room to turn without brushing against warm skin covered by wet clothes and hair swinging like intricate ropes and a hard body that was still soft enough, vulnerable enough to hold. He stood near the bathtub, the lilac rug darkening, shifting shape and color beneath his feet.

"Let me get you a towel." The linen closet was hidden in a small corner, directly across from the toilet. She placed a red towel in his hands, noticed that his mouth trembled slightly, teeth sinking into the lower lip to prevent chattering. "Take a hot shower."

"No, no, I don't want to impose on you like that. I can dry off and just be on my way." The weight of his hair seemed to pull his head down. She placed both hands on either side of his head and she was immediately confronted with women's eyes in a man's tough, intense face.

"Please. You're freezing. Take a shower, rinse out your hair and I'll find you some sweats to wear and throw your clothes in the dryer. Please."

"Okay. Okay, I'll take a shower, then."

She let him go and left the bathroom.

There was panic on the other side of the door, the wood supported the whole of her body, one hand on the knob and the other pressing against her chest, measuring the alarming rate of heartbeats and imagining the man behind the closed door who was always there, even when he wasn't following her, stripping off his clothes and stepping into her shower.

Her heartbeat was slowing, her hand relaxed its tightness against the doorknob, the panic ebbing, and she tried to control her breathing and visualize calm, still waters and heard the shower pouring like rain outside from the bathroom. She knew that he was standing beneath the spray, the wave of his hair heavy and hanging down past his waist and dark skin gleaming and shining, reflecting all the light that ever was and his eyes closed and the chill seeping slowly out of his skin.

She found him a pair of old sweatpants and a huge T-shirt that wasn't hers and she couldn't figure out who they belonged to, which man had left them and why. She'd had the sweatpants for almost two years, liked to wear them on lazy Sunday or Saturday afternoons, feel the frayed fabric rubbing against her skin and the waistline hanging loose around her hips, but there was no name, no face that she could possibly conjure up, just a steady stream of men staying and leaving stuff behind that sometimes she threw away and sometimes she kept and none of it really making a difference to her. Men talking about Black Liberation and Black Power and helping her forget where and who she had been. Men needed in the middle of the night when all that went before caught up with her and there was no way around it or through it except through dark skin and dark hands and firm, mobile mouths. Men needed in the middle of the night and hoping, praying that her child didn't know or didn't mind and that she wasn't doing any damage that couldn't be hugged and kissed away. They were all so broken, living and dying inside, even as she held them, let them come into her, bodies moving against hers, she smelled death on the breath, burial earth in the hair, a coolness about the flesh. Just that was enough to send them home the next day, nothing more, no mistakes or apologies or sly promises, just the scent and the smell and the touch of something rotting.

She was afraid, at times, that it would rub off on her, she wondered how she could ignore the walking dead for the sake of limited pleasure or newness, the hope of a bit more and it all felt the same when she closed her eyes. Eyes closed and she couldn't remember if it were Teddy or Salah or Hakim or Mike, the smells, the hands roaming her body, the pleasures were all the same and the next morning waking up with these men in her bed she simply felt tired. Sent them on their way with kisses and smiles that reached the eyes but didn't quite reach the heart and spent the day with her child and the evenings in the studio frantic and determined to give birth to something after an evening spent digging up graves and pretending that she could breathe life back into numb limbs.

The sweatpants and the T-shirt were folded neatly in one arm and she stood outside of the bathroom door and again felt her heart pounding and the shortness of breath and panic racing in. The shower went off abruptly, she took a few deep breaths and knocked firmly. "Taji? Taji, I have the sweats for you and the T-shirt."

The door opened fully and he was standing there in a towel and the length of his hair in a knot at the top of his head and so much water coming down from him that his body looked as if it were sobbing and yards of steam billowing out behind him. His scent, frankincense, blending with her peppermint soap and the ash and the cold no longer hounding his skin.

"Thanks. You have no idea how good that felt."

The door closed and she sat down on the throw rug in the hallway, in the midst of Imani's dolls and her women, waiting for him. The dolls stared at her intently and she randomly stroked their hair and soft, plush limbs. "I wonder when Imani's going to get over being angry and let you all back in?" she whispered. "You all just can't stay out here, tripping people." The dolls were silent and she tried to imagine the conversations that they had with Imani, tried to recall her own girlhood when dolls were her best friends and she stayed up late into the night, dolls piled upon her bed, giggling and talking low enough so that she wouldn't wake Lilly.

Taji came out of the bathroom, the towel that had been wrapped about his body now tied like a turban about his head, hiding all that hair from sight. The sweatpants and T-shirt that fit loose on her were tight on him and patches of damp had the clothes clinging randomly to different parts of his body. She always thought of him as small, but now when there was nothing against his skin but the clothes she had given him, she could see that men and women carried smallness differently. He was compact and wiry and strong, she never thought of him as strong, and so slim because he didn't carry any fat just lean muscle, bone and all that smooth dark skin.

He laughed at her. "You look like Imani sitting there, surrounded by all those dolls, only your eyes and your hair peeking out. Why are they all scattered in the hallway, any-way?"

She shrugged, smiled, motioned for him to join her on

the floor, laughed when he had to fight cloth bodies to find a space on the throw rug. "They had a falling out with Imani."

"Really?"

"That's what she told me."

"You know what happened?"

"Something about the bed and she wasn't sleeping on the floor for nobody. And then the dolls caught an attitude with her, you know how dolls can be, and she kicked them all out. She did that yesterday, while she was packing an overnight bag to go to Violet's. She didn't want any of them getting in her bed as soon as she left."

He picked up a doll, ran his finger over a dark mouth and fake gem eyes. "You didn't make her clean it up?"

"No, they don't bother me and sometimes I'm so tickled by the things Imani does. You should have seen her bringing each doll out one by one, but she wouldn't put them on the floor, she made sure they had a spot on the rug so I'm betting that she'll move them all back in when she comes home. In any case, they provide my women with some much-needed company." Her racing heart and shortness of breath and chasing panic were gone, she was easy and absently began to separate and twist her hair.

"You are such a good mother."

Her hands stilled and she turned to gaze at him, she could feel his warmth through the mountain of dolls. With the towel tied around his head he was unbearably pretty, his eyes huge, his skin smooth, and faint stubble dusting his chin and cheeks. "You think so?"

"Yeah, I do. I thought so when I first met Imani. Lilly was

a mess and here was this beautiful little girl with all this light and laughter."

"People always talk about how hard it is raising kids. When I first got pregnant I was almost dumb with fear because I had to do it alone and I had no idea how to do anything but make women and how was that going to feed a child? But almost from the first, when I first started to feel her inside of me, Imani was a gift."

He took the towel off his head and his hair gradually fell down his back. He squeezed it out, section by section, with the towel. "It must be something, huh? Loving someone that much? Shit, just knowing that you're capable of it must be something."

"I guess it is . . ." He was finished with the towel but she could still see drops of water clinging stubbornly to his locks. "I have a blow-dryer. I can dry your hair for you, if you want."

He smiled at her and she remembered Imani telling her that he was one of the prettiest things that she had ever seen. "That sounds good, but I don't feel like moving."

She stretched, preparing to get up, pushing dolls out of her way. "We don't have to go too far, just to the bathroom." She rose, held out a hand to him; he gingerly took it and pulled himself to his feet and she felt the calluses of his palms against her own, marks of a worker or an artist or both and she wondered what he did other than being a Black Panther or ex–Black Panther like all the Black Panthers were now, 1976 and all the Black Panthers going or gone like almost everyone else.

"I think I stepped on someone's head by accident," he

said, smiling, and she laughed as she led him back into the bathroom.

"Have a seat on the toilet." She dug the hair dryer out from the cabinet beneath the sink.

"Your house smells like you."

"You think?" she asked, plugged the dryer in and prepared to get to work.

"Yeah. Smells like lavender and peppermint and warm bread and herbal tea, and roses, I couldn't forget the roses."

"It's funny isn't it? Mama named me after my favorite scent, little did she know." Her hands traveled over the length of his hair, lost themselves in the damp and darkness and the blond ends. "It's so soft. I didn't expect it to be so soft, like a child's head. How long have you been growing them?" Her heart jump-started, the breath stuttered, the panic reared impatiently, and she pictured herself perfumed and hair braided and bejeweled for him.

"About eight years, before I moved from New York to come down here."

"Lilly's been growing hers for about eight years, too. Mama nearly fainted when she first started, went around mumbling about her looking like a vagabond. But she likes them now."

"You see Lilly a lot? I mean, she comes over and visits you?"

"No, she's too busy doing what she's into and it's far too painful for me, anyhow."

"I have a sister out there like that. My baby sister running through New York doing God knows what for a hit. My mom kicked her out, stealing and all that bullshit, but whenever I go home I look for her. Man. Man, when I say it's always a fucking blow to see her, to see this wasted, fucked-up junkie and try to find my sister, who was this beautiful girl, in the middle of all that mess."

"That's the hard part, isn't it? Trying to find the person they had been or trying to hold on to them like they were. I never think of Lilly shooting up. When I think of her we're both girls sharing the same room and she is the light of my life. Literally the light of my life, I swear, I have never seen a more beautiful human being than her. I thought she was some kind of angel, you know? But Lord God how she has fallen."

He raised his head to her, eyes steady and wondering. "Baby, don't you know that we are all going to fall, that we have all fallen? And now, it's just a matter of digging our way out of this hole of shit that we somehow stumbled into."

She switched off the hair dryer, laid it on the side of the sink, ran her hands over his almost-dry hair, let them still at his crown. "Why do you follow me? Why are you with me everywhere I go? I should think that you're crazy, insane, should probably call the cops or someone on you but I don't think you're any of those things. I don't. And that makes me wonder if maybe I'm the crazy one. Maybe I'm simply out of my mind to look over my shoulder and be happy that you're there, even though you don't say a word, never a word."

"Rose. Rose," he said and nothing more and she was left floundering, trying to make sense of it all.

"I think of you at night, you know? At night when I'm

alone and tired from a long day, after I've kissed my child and put her to bed, I think of you. I wonder what your day was like, when you weren't following me, of course. And I imagine how it would be if you were with me so that maybe we could talk about it. And I wonder how I can think anything at all about you when you don't talk, just follow."

He stood and her hands fell to her sides as she looked up at him. "I love you."

She almost laughed, certainly took a step back, considered. "You have no idea what you're saying. You can't mean that. You can't because you don't know me the same way that I don't know you. I don't even know what you do for a living."

"I'm a writer, I write to eat. And I know you, God, I know you."

She shook her head. "No, no don't you come at me like that . . ."

"I'm not trying to . . . Listen. Listen. You are so completely beautiful. All this dark brown skin, and hair braided or out and strong reaching up, always up. You are this incredible mother, your daughter is happy and always smiling and aware of her own worth, but that's not it. You're an artist, a woman who creates other women and I see your work in galleries and in your home and I'm so moved by your faces and bodies and hands that tell stories that were never meant to be told, but that's not it. The first time I saw you, the very first time I knew. It was as simple as that, and I know it sounds crazy and corny and I really don't give a shit. I'm not asking you to spend time with me or love me or marry me or even sleep with me. I just want you to know that I love you. So I guess that's why I follow you when I can, because I know and knowing, I swear, I don't want to let you out of my sight."

She stood there, mouth opened, hands limp at her sides, and the panic almost blinding her. "What? How am I suppose to respond to that? What do you want me to say?"

"I'm sorry. Sorry, this is all wrong. The way . . . It's all wrong." He was moving away from her, the pink of his tongue showing through parted lips, and his woman's eyes wandering desperately about the small bathroom.

"Wait. Just wait a minute. You can't come and say all that and then tell me it's wrong and make a mad dash for the door. Taji, you can't pull shit like that on people." He stilled, his mouth closed and he watched her. "I don't know how to respond to everything you said. I'm not sure if I believe that you love me because it makes absolutely no sense, and you know it. Look, you said that you don't want to marry me or sleep with me or spend time. And I don't want to marry you either, but the rest, Taji. I would really, really like all the rest, to lay with you and roam together and see what happens. I want that."

She went to him, wrapped her slender, sturdy arms about his neck, felt his heavy hair against her skin, placed gentle kisses across his face.

His hands went to her hair, the thickness and the nappiness and the warmth of her scalp. "I . . ."

"Hush, baby, just hush . . ."

Death was not hounding him like the others since Charles, there was no burial earth in his hair, no scent of something rotten upon his breath; there was no need for her to breathe life into his limbs, no searching for warmth against cool skin. He was hot, so hot and his breath was sweet, scented with honey and she eagerly took him in, the taste of honey and lemon and salt, the red insides of his mouth burning, scalding her skin. Sheets that smelled of rose and lavender incense clinging to damp skin even as they clung to each other, not two bodies at the center of the universe, nothing so romantic, especially since she didn't believe in romance. There was nothing in scented sheets and darkness and heat with a man who had locks down to his waist to fear or hold back or keep hidden. The heart that was her room beating at a steady, intense pace unlike the heart of her insides, a stuttering heart, strong and weak and beating in tandem with the touch and withdrawal of his hands, the long length of his body. His body covering her and moving over her or lying still against her, absorbing the softness and wet of her skin. There was a lightness in her stomach, between her thighs, encircling her neck and head, a drifting even though she was seeped in texture and taste and smell. His hair wrapped about her as if it were an extension of his body, the intricate ropes gently scratching or caressing her breasts, her sides, the length of her spine. The moistness of his breath and tongue against the back of her knees, her inner elbows, her lower back. He kept her with him, his rough hands, the hands of a worker or artist or fighter, keeping her quiet and shuddering and dazed.

Studio Time

UNCUT WOOD AND STONE LINED THE WALLS, gleamed beneath the reflection of glass and light in the windowsill, laid out before her on her workbench. Her hands wanted to move, really. If not carve and chisel and shape, at least move over the smooth paper with pencil and sketch. Her hands lay throbbing at her sides in impatience as she twirled slowly and aimlessly about on her workbench. A creative block, a creative distraction, a shutdown of nerve signals from brain to arm and hand and she simply could not work. She tried to get at the heart of the distraction, to pull and pick at her feelings and emotions, laying them all neatly before her to fix whatever it was that needed fixing.

There was so much going on, so much new feeling, and new experience, and new touch and taste. Wood and stone solid and offering her the possibility of creation and in her head she was still in her bedroom with Taji, the red walls pulsing like blood, like the blood moving rapidly beneath her skin and muscle. His hair spread out across her sheets and pillow, his heat rising to meet her, his elegant man's body open to her. Taji sitting on her bed, utterly naked and vulnerable. His hair long and thick and nappy, his eyes glazed and wet.

"Please," he said to her from the bed. "Please, just come here and let me hold you."

She stared at him, at the absolute dark of his skin, beautiful skin, always healthy and glowing. Skin like a child, only the underlying hardness hinting that he was a man. His eyes were wide and deep, woman's eyes. His mouth was trembling, as if he were fighting back tears.

"Please," he said. "Please."

His body was tense, and she could feel his heat from where she was standing. He wanted to fuck her, he wanted to love her. His penis was rigid. She knew its length and texture, its taste and smell. His body hair was soft and dense, it covered his chest, his legs, his pubic area.

She took him down, down to cool sheets, wrapped herself around him. When he reached for her she shook her head and whispered, "No, let me." She placed his arms above his head, and moved away from him. She ran her fingers over the fragile softness of his mouth and his tongue followed the light touch. She was water moving over him and against him, an unceasing ebb and flow. Sweat on his body and she drank it from his skin, enjoying the salt and the sweet, the taste of him.

"Please," he said. "Please."

Her mouth against the inside of his thigh and his entire body arched.

Her hands greedily gathered him to her. Her mouth trailed down to the back of his knee. She lingered over the arch of his foot, the curve of his ankle, the swell of his calf, the dense hair between his thighs. She turned him upon his stomach and ran her lips down his spine.

His back was supple, muscles beneath her hands and lips bunched and flexed. She felt the trembling, the humming of his body. She was making his body sing. She placed her cheek against his back to hear him better. Her body rested on sheets damp with their sweat.

She rolled completely on top of him, face resting in the cradle of his neck, breasts against his back. His breathing was heavy and shallow. She paced her breath to his and their bodies moved in rhythm. Her hands sweeping the long length of his locks to the side, tongue tracing the fine hairs at the base of his neck and the shell of his ear.

He turned and shifted, placing his full weight against her. His hands in her hair and his face at her neck. She was bearing his weight, holding him up. His hands at her waist, his fingers digging into tender skin. She rose to meet his heat, rose to meet his mouth, rose to meet him. He was solid, solid and dense.

He turned on his back with her and she straddled him. Her hair a large Afro on her head, back straight, brown legs on either side of him. His hands spread carelessly above his head and he was staring at her, searching, digging, searching for her center. She moved deliberately and slowly and Taji squeezed his eyes shut.

"My God," he said.

She was flying, flying every night since he first touched

her. And the skies were clear and blue and the sun scorching hot, her body, their bodies traveling across time and space without leaving the red of her bedroom. She couldn't think through the pleasure, couldn't concentrate, could only walk around smiling and waiting for time alone with him at night, waiting for a touch like she had never been touched before. Waiting for him to say "please" and "I love you" because with him "please" wasn't an imposition or demand and she almost believed that he loved her. Body and nerves and emotions dazed at his touch and her hands simply did not want to create women, to touch wood and stone, not when they could be touching him.

Taji

H E HAD A WOMAN, a magic woman, that he couldn't get off his mind. Magic woman binding him to her with the rhythms and measures of her body. Taji would have never thought that a woman was like a song, that her body, her mind sang haunting or joyous or sad melodies and all he had to do was listen, just sit and listen and let the music take him inside of her, inside of himself. Finding himself through the arms and smiles and laughter and cycles of a woman.

He sat quietly sometimes, trying to make himself invisible, upon the floor of Rose's studio, and watched her work. Her body relaxed and fluid, her hands moving swiftly and precisely across charcoal sketches or the smooth or rough surface of wood and stone. Small hands, a woman's long fingers, the nails cut short and the brown skin nicked and cut and permanently scarred and palms callused from years of reincarnating ancestors. The depth of her work was surprising, women singing the blues, women with babies at the breast, women taking care of white people's children, women in their lovers' arms, women who drank too much or had marks lining their arms, women in the process of giving birth to themselves, women with bruised eyes and busted lips from a lover's fist, women bent over in pain and standing tall with confidence and vulnerability about the mouth and eyes.

This woman whom he shared his nights with, long nights spent touching and talking and refiguring the world, this woman whom he spent his days with, holding her and her child with a tenderness, a kindness that he hadn't realized was in him, knew all about vulnerability. It was there in the way she treated her child, recognizing that harsh words could not only hurt, but kill; the way she treated him, constantly willing to share pieces of herself without imposing or demanding that he give anything that he did not have. No superwoman lived inside of her, she was not the backbone of the race and she did not have to carry the weight of the world. He did not have to try and be superman for her, for the first time in all his dealings with women—brown and black and red and pale and golden women with slender or round soft bodies, with no hair or hair that curled to their waist or hair that reached for the sky—all he had to be was himself, and he was discovering who that self was within the red heart of her bedroom, the steady beating of her kindness and care.

The days, nights, weeks that he spent at her house, watching her work, cooking her breakfast and dinner, reading and playing with Imani were a revelation for him, a woman's scent constantly moving around him, inside him. A revelation after a miserable year spent fighting in Vietnam, brown bodies on both sides riddled by bullets and men carrying fingers and ears like prized possessions, like they were on some exotic hunt, raping women and children indiscriminately. Waking up in a jungle in the middle of Asia and knowing that he wasn't supposed to be there, facing the blistering heat of the day, green and pulsing and wet, and feeling his conscience slip away, away into the mud and the foliage and villages and shifting hillsides.

Then it was over, nothing won and everything lost, and he was sent home, they all were sent home, fingers and ears, trophies, burning holes in their pockets. It wasn't until they hit American soil that they had time to reconsider, reconsider and wonder and falter under the shame, the confusion of just following orders and all the good lost. The dreams and the nightmares, waking up in a cold sweat and running to the bathroom to empty the stomach and bladder, laying a damp face against cool tiles and praying for all of it to stop.

Coming home he was a mess, an absolute mess, realizing that they taught him how to fight, how to kill, but not how to fight or kill for anything important. He had to learn it all over, standing in unemployment lines fighting for work because not many people wanted to hire a Vietnam vet, not one with sadness and meanness and desperation still creeping about the eyes and the mouth, not one whose hands were constantly balled into fists, constantly ready to pound flesh for the casual insult, the wrong word, the wrong tone of voice, a bump against the shoulder. Standing on neighborhood corners, stiff and braced against the junkies, the pimps, the hustlers, all trying to get over, get paid, get high, get fucked at someone else's expense. Bracing himself against the effortlessness of surrender, of wandering street corners and robbing and raping and conning older women who looked like his mother, young girls who reminded him of his sister, brothers with faces like all the brothers in Vietnam who didn't make it home, bodies still rotting in heat and dark earth and miles away from family or anyone who actually gave a fuck.

There was no money and all the heroes retired and people talking about the movement like it was over, like the only thing black people had to worry about was the vote and the rest would take care of itself. All the time hot rage, hot rage moving inside of him and cleaning him out, rage that allowed him to dig, to go back to that land and those people that he had wronged and find his conscience, his lost self. He went to his closet, dug in the pockets of his old uniform and retrieved fingers and ears wrinkled with time and losing color and the stench was ripe and full, reminding him of the stench of the jungle after rain or months with no rain, jungle rotting and thriving and trying to make everything near its borders part of soaring tree, tangled green, and gaping earth.

Wrapping human body parts in colorful silk scarves, blue and green and orange and purple, from his mama's closet and putting it all to rest. Strolling down cement sidewalks, his package securely under one arm and trying to remember faces, who did the finger with the ring belong to, or the ear with a slashed lobe? He could only recall blood and sightless, open eyes watching him as he pulled out his knife, thinking, *We are all going to die, every last one of us is going to die here and now.*

Carrying the box into the neighborhood bar, Champagne's, finding a lone table in the back and ordering a pitcher of beer, toasting all the dead left in Vietnam. He started drinking at three in the afternoon and wasn't done until ten that night. He still didn't get everyone, knew that there were men in his platoon that he couldn't remember, countless Vietnamese and American soldiers that he simply didn't know.

He was drunk by the time he left, good and drunk and sweet with it. Helping women carry late evening groceries into the house while their sons ran wild, buying a starving junkie a burger and some fries from McDonald's, rescuing a prostitute from a persistent, unwanted john. The silk orange and purple and blue and green scarves wrapped tenderly about fingers and ears still in the box and secure beneath his arm. He reached the graveyard around midnight. Midnight and people shouting and cursing and partying up and down the streets, young guys on corners lighting up joints and passing bottles, young women sitting on their steps with hair and nails and makeup done and laughing, flirting smiles.

The graveyard was still, he just walked right in. He found a clear patch of grass beneath a large, looming tree. He went to his knees, like he was praying, like he was a boy and at the foot of his bed with his mama standing over him. The damp seeped through his jeans, cold against warm skin, reminding him of cool rain that fell in the jungle or the hot blood of a Vietnamese man, woman, or child against his flesh.

His hands were digging, furiously digging, pulling away tufts of grass and clawing at hard ground, hands like pickaxes and shovels constantly moving. Dirt in his face, dirt in his hair, dirt clinging to his forearms and hands and piling in front of him and to the side of him. His fingernails broke, bled, blood mixing with the dirt like Vietnam where the earth was permanently stained, blood nourishing the foliage of the jungle like water and sunlight. He was crying, deep, heavy sobs, the liquor and the waste leaking from his eyes, falling upon his hands.

There was a gaping, deep hole in front of him and he was gasping for breath, chest heaving and hands numb. He knew that he must look like a madman, dirt-covered and anxious and eyes wet and ferocious. He picked up the box gingerly, the weight and the smoothness easy in his hands. There was no sense in it, no matter how he turned and twisted and tried to approach it from a different way, there was no sense in it.

He placed the shoe box in the hole and covered it, shoving dirt with long, sweeping gestures, getting caught up in the rhythm, the ritual of death. There were no rituals in Vietnam, they simply left bodies where they fell, cautiously or hastily stepped over friend and enemy alike. There were no people in Vietnam, just carcasses, and they left them exposed to suffocating humidity and glaring heat, limbs torn and blown off, cut away to make a charm for someone's neck.

The shoe box was covered; the ground packed and loose, like a dog had been digging for a bone or a shoe. He sat still for a second, trying to feel the weight of it all leaving his back, looking up at the sky and then to his own bloodied hands. He lay down on the wet earth, over the makeshift grave and at the base of the tree. He was still there in the morning, opening bleeding eyes to a group of schoolchildren throwing small pebbles at him, feeling the pebbles nick softly at the skin of his face and arms and not moving until they grew bored and went on their way.

He walked home, covered in dirt and damp and nothing changed. He thought that he could get rid of the memories, empty out his head, be the person he was before the war. He needed that boy because all he had was a man who was a part-time drunk and a possible junkie trying to find, to hold on to the good, and in danger of doing anything to anybody at anytime.

He walked into the house and thanked God that his mama had already left for work and his sister for school. They would have stared at him, just stared at him for a moment and then spoke quietly and got him out of his clothes and into bed like he was sick. His mama had left him a breakfast of scrambled eggs, grits, pork sausage, and biscuits warming on the stove and he sat at the kitchen table and wolfed it down. Wolfed it down silently like he was stopping for a break with his platoon and had to be quiet so that he could hear all sounds, hearing to stay alive. He stumbled up the stairs, tracking dirt on his mother's new carpet and telling himself to clean it up before she came home from work and falling into bed and sleeping the sleep of a soldier, ignoring the aches and pains of his body and the wet of his clothes against his rough skin, spreading into clean bed linen.

Taji stood in the doorway of Rose's small kitchen and watched her as she cooked. Hands deft and careful as she cleaned and cut collard greens, like she was still in her studio and shaping women with precision and gut instinct. The kidney beans were already on the stove, thick steam smelling of spicy seasoning batting against Rose's face and making her hair curl as she leaned against the countertop near the stove. The fish was in the oven, the heads and tails still on, smothered in onion and fresh, ripe tomato, almost done.

She turned to him, smiled, winked. "What you staring at?"

Her face, shining with sweat and steam and curling, nappy hair was so pretty and alive and good. All the good that he ever needed right there in her smile. "You. I'm staring at you."

Her grin widened. "Yeah?"

He crossed the kitchen to her, wrapped his arms about her waist, placed his lips at her neck, breathing in the peppermint of her hair and the rose oil on her skin. "Yeah, you. You are the most beautiful woman, the most beautiful woman . . ."

She pulled slightly away from him, watched his face; he knew that she was looking for some kind of truth, that sometimes she still tried to figure out the how and why instead of just letting go. He kissed her, placed his lips against that deliciously brown, mobile mouth and drew her to him. She came easily, like the first night they made love. He took in all her good, single mother, daughter, sister, artist, fighter, friend, lover and gave it back to her, gave it back to her so that she could taste the good on his tongue, hunt for it in the red warmth of his mouth, smell it on his breath.

He withdrew, placed his mouth back on her neck, on the space where shoulder and collarbone connected, took all of her weight. "I love you."

She was puzzled, he could see it in her face, a little girl's wonder and confusion. "You don't have to say that, you know?"

"I know. I do. I say it because I mean it and not because I want or need you to say anything in return. It's not like that. It's not conditional and there's no pressure on you to feel anything but what you're feeling."

She smiled, searched for the smooth skin of his back beneath his shirt. "Okay. Okay, I won't feel anything but what I feel and we'll go from there."

"That's fine, baby. That is so fine with me."

She playfully pushed him away from her. "Go. Get out and let me finish cooking my dinner. Go see what Imani's doing."

He left, walking through the house that smelled of Rose and Imani and was full of colors and wood and stone women staring down at him from every corner, from all angles. It was the first time in his life that he was so completely in a woman's space. Vietnam was all men; after he came home and was able to get himself together he joined the Black Panther Party and that was a space of men, even though women were a part of the whole thing, he never felt their presence, not with so much testosterone out of control. The Panthers got him thinking and working as a freelance writer and out of New York and down to Philly. It was while he was working on the newsletter for the Panthers that he dis-

174

covered that he could write, that he liked it, that it helped him make sense out of a world where people were shooting up and zoning out, living below the poverty line, selling themselves or anything that they get their hands on to eat, hunger like a knife in the belly.

Studio Time

S HE WAS WORKING on a piece about sisters, carved in wood, hands and legs and arms the same and different, sisters born of the same form, taking the same shape and still peculiarities. Three sisters carved in dark wood, standing tall from the same base, limbs intertwined and holding on to each other, brown strong slender limbs. The faces different and similar, same eyes, familiarity about the mouth and nose, but the expressions different and changing. Sometimes quiet and thoughtful, sometimes bright and alert, sometimes distracted and worried and all the expressions telling a story about sisters and sisterhood that she was all the time trying to get just right. All the time trying to figure out what did it mean to grow up in a house full of black women when being black and woman wasn't something that anyone else really wanted to be.

The eyes, it was in the eyes. Always that black woman's knowledge behind the eyes, the knowledge passed through generations, passed from mother to daughter and mother to daughter, the knowledge that she was trying to pass on to Imani. Knowledge that wasn't specific or general, always becoming something different and something new, depending upon the woman. She knew, was all the time learning that being black and woman was just as complex and just as difficult and just as individual and just as collective as being anything or anyone else—no easy answers at all.

When she was little she was all the time looking for herself in Mama's face and the faces of her sisters, all the time wondering why and how she was both daughter and sister and friend. She thought for the longest time that they were all the same person, all the same person just different faces and different ways of being in the world. It was okay that Violet was so mean and Lilly always talking to spirits and she was always drawing or thinking about drawing because Mama was solid and they were all the same. All the same and that meant that she had Violet's meanness and Lilly's way of not really being in the world and Mama's solidness in her, too.

She shared a room with Lilly and Violet had her own room but they all slept together sometimes. Together on Violet's bed with Violet in the center and she and Lilly curled into Violet's sides. Violet warm and pretty and dark like Mama and the oldest and for a long time Rose was constantly wanting all the time to sit in her lap, all the time have some part of her body touching Violet.

Violet's room was small and the walls were painted in quiet greens and Violet didn't have dolls all over her bed the way that she and Lilly had dolls all the time sleeping with them or huddled at the foot of the bed beneath the covers. Violet was too old for dolls, had already started thinking about boys and makeup by the time that Daddy died.

Sleeping with both her sisters and talking real low so Mama wouldn't come around and hush them. Violet's bedroom nighttime quiet and Violet's dolls watching and listening to them from the chair in the corner or the top of Violet's dresser. Dolls looking so lonely and so cold that Rose always wanted to bring them to bed but Violet insisted that having to sleep with two little sisters was enough without adding fake gem eyes and fake yarn hair. Violet's bed and room smelling like the too-sweet perfume that she had already begun to dab at her wrists, neck, and knees. Violet patient with her because she was the youngest and what did she know? And impatient with Lilly because Lilly was always somewhere else. Sometimes they talked about their friends, or school, or dolls, or books. Sometimes they talked about Daddy and death.

"Why you think God took Daddy?"

"It was just his time to go, that's all, Rose." Violet was the oldest and tried to talk like Mama talked and be the way that Mama was when Mama wasn't around.

"What does that mean, though?" She wished that Violet would talk like a little girl so that she could understand her some.

"It means that God wanted him with him."

"Oh. Well, I wanted him with us, Violet."

"Yeah, me, too."

"God didn't take Daddy," Lilly said.

Violet hushed her. "Be quiet, Lilly."

"No. God didn't take Daddy."

"Okay. Since you know so much, if God didn't take Daddy, what happened?" Violet asked, frustrated with Lilly and Lilly's ways.

"He left. That's all. Daddy just left."

"Without saying good-bye?" Rose asked.

"Shut up, Lilly," Violet said.

"He left without saying anything at all," Lilly said.

Phone Conversation

"MAMA?"

"Lilly, I'm not going to do this with you anymore. I told you that."

"No 'where you at' or 'when you coming home,' Mama?"

"Oh, Lilly . . . We keep doing this and getting nowhere and I just refuse to keep on going like this. I'm here whenever you're ready to get some help or let someone help you but until then I can't do anything for you."

"Do you want to know where I am?"

"If you want to tell me."

"It doesn't matter, really. Listen, I been thinking about when I used to write you poetry. You remember that?"

"Of course I do, Lilly. I still have all the poems you gave me."

"I was thinking about it because I was always trying to give you something. You always worked so hard and never complained and never even really looked tired even though

180

I know you must have been all the time exhausted. All the time tired like I'm all the time tired and I don't have any three little people staring and depending and leaning on me . . ."

"You all were what I wanted, Lilly, that's all."

"I know, Mama. I was all the time writing you poetry because I knew that even when I was little. I wanted to give you something and words and paper were all I had. All I've ever had."

"Why did you stop writing, Lilly? You were good, everyone said so, your teachers and all."

"You know what, Mama? One day I woke up and my skin was red, bright blood red and paper-thin. So you know what I did? I just peeled it back, peeled the skin of my belly right off, and you know what I found?"

"I can't do this, Lilly. I think that you're not high and we can have some kind of talk and then you start on . . . Is there ever a moment when you're not high, baby? Because if there is . . . Listen very carefully. If there is, only talk to me when you're not high. Only call me and only come home when you haven't been shooting up. I don't want to know you like this anymore."

"I found whole worlds, Mama. Whole worlds precisely mapped beneath my skin in green ink. Green ink, of all things!"

"Good-bye, baby . . ."

"Wait, Mama! Wait!"

"What?"

"They were worlds of pain, Mama. Worlds of pain

mapped beneath my skin and there were no words to describe it and if there were no words to describe it that meant . . . You know what that meant?"

"Good-bye. Love you."

"It meant that there were no words at all."

Imani

A UNT LILLY'S CHILDHOOD ROOM was like a tomb, an ancient tribal burial ground but there was no earth or grass or sky just white walls covered in pictures torn from newspapers and magazines, wanted posters ripped from the waiting rooms of sterilized government offices. There was no light, shades and curtains drawn tight even though it was early afternoon Saturday, and raging candles placed carelessly on the night table and floor and the dull edges beneath the window. Pictures and posters of black and brown and yellow people running and screaming and fighting and crying and in so much pain that it was hard for Imani to take it all in without her childhood slipping from the edges of her gaze, leaking like tears from eyes that were absolutely dry. Aunt Lilly sat in the middle of it all, scissors in hand, diligently cutting out more pictures.

Aunt Lilly being buried alive and no fear, no fear of the dark, or the ground, becoming a part of the Earth easy in the heart with calm breath. Aunt Lilly tuning out Grandma's threats and worry, tuning out Mommy's tears and pleas, tuning out Aunt Violet's demands and letting everything go. Aunt Lilly wanting the quiet and the stillness of the grave. Grave and silence and darkness and falling apart on the insides because that's what Mommy and Grandma said happened to people once they died—they fell apart on the insides. First the insides stopped, no beating blood or pulsing heart or nerves racing through the brain, and then they became soft. The skin became so soft that it could be pulled away and eventually fell from the muscle and bone all by itself. The heart and the liver and the bladder so soft that they were almost like jelly, slipping and sliding through bone, leaking into the ground, everything leaking until there was only bone and nothing else. There must be a smell when things fall apart, when everything goes soft and then leaks away. Maybe the smell of damp green things on a rainy day or Mommy's wood when she first cut it open to make women or the smell of the bathroom each month when Mommy bled.

Imani stepped fully into the room, shutting the door behind her, shutting out the smell of Grandma's cooking coming from the kitchen downstairs, shutting in the smell of Aunt Lilly's incense and air that was old and needed washing.

"Aunt Lilly? What you doing?"

Aunt Lilly looked up at her, her smile came slow across her face, her eyes sunken in her head and crinkling at the corners.

"Hey, darling mine. What you doing here?" It was a question, but not really because as soon as she asked she went back to cutting, scissors moving precisely, bottom lip caught between her teeth.

"I'm here for the day to see you and Grandma." Imani didn't mention that Grandma had told her that she couldn't stay in Aunt Lilly's room long because there was no telling what Aunt Lilly would do at any given time especially when she was running the streets like she didn't have a brain in her head and hanging pictures of dead people on her walls.

Aunt Lilly looked back up at her, smiled. "Just for the day, huh? Well, come help me then."

"You got an extra pair of scissors?"

"Look in the night table drawer."

Imani went to the night table, stepping carefully over the pictures that Aunt Lilly had scattered across the floor, pictures that she was sure couldn't fit anywhere on the walls. "Aunt Lilly, where are all these going to go?"

"The ceiling."

"But how are you going to get up there?"

"Mama got a ladder in the basement, as soon as I have enough pictures I'll bring the ladder up."

"But why?"

"Get the scissors and come help me and I'll tell you about it."

Imani pulled the night table drawer open and there were nothing but scissors. Scissors in every shape and size, some with dull edges, some with edges that looked so sharp that she was afraid to touch them, afraid that they might draw blood. She sat cross-legged on the floor, her knee touching the skin and bone of Aunt Lilly's thigh.

Aunt Lilly handed her a magazine. "Cut out pictures

only of people who look like you. And when you cut try to think about their lives, okay?"

"What do you mean?"

"I mean try to imagine what their lives must be like from the picture. You know, sometimes people look sad or happy or scared. Think about what the picture is trying to tell you when you cut it out."

"Why do you have them all over the place? Why are you doing this?"

Aunt Lilly stilled, dropped the scissors, stared at Imani as if she were the only person in the world who made any kind of sense. "Oh child, little girl child walking easy in the world. I think you know everything about it and nothing about it."

Imani sat still, trying to take it all in, most of it going over her head so that she was left with just the question: "Why?"

Aunt Lilly laughed lightly. "I forgot. Silly me, I forgot that you wanted an answer. Darling mine, I don't think I have one. Not one that's going to do either of us or anyone the least bit of good but each night I dream the same dream. Each and every night no matter where I end up sleeping or who I end up sleeping with or how tired I am, I have the same dream."

"What kind of dream?"

"I am walking through time. Just strolling back through history and watching everything go by so slow, and I can't speed it up, can't move or walk faster or run. I just stroll and at first I'm moving through cities, places that look like here and that's okay because I know these places. I know all about row houses and tar streets and cat piss in alleyways and tall buildings and everyone constantly going and everyone constantly sad and constantly biting off their tongues to keep from screaming. And that's just fine with me because I've spent my whole life in the streets, and once you let go it's not so bad. Not the worst thing at all, just letting the body and mind become like water so that you can reshape yourself around the blows, fit yourself about the beatings.

"I visit all my usual places but the people are different. There isn't one familiar face and you know I don't even care. I just want to feel that needle, baby. I just want to hold that strap of leather in my mouth and feel that sweet piercing of skin and fly. I don't care who's watching and I certainly don't care if friends aren't there. I hold the belt between my teeth and tongue and place the needle against my skin and my blood turns to fire. I look down and see my hand on fire, feel fire shooting from the top of my head, fire coming from underneath my dress and between my thighs and this hurts, hurts so bad that I almost pass out and I can't understand it because I'm water and nothing can hurt water.

"I am still burning and I try to get up and run but I can only walk slowly and everyone, all these people that I have never seen before, turn to stare at me and none of them will help me.

"Finally, I walk into the country. I'm in the South, not too far from where Daddy's from and there is this cool, light rain falling and it puts out the fire. I can smell the sea nearby and hear the faint lapping of waves against distant shores. My skin is smoking and all this steam is rising up off me and all my hair is gone but I'm not burned anywhere, just bald-headed. There's all this green around me, the smell of my bubble baths and I can look up and see the sky. My clothes are a little scorched and I'm standing on this old dirt road and I start walking again. All these brown golden black yellow people are walking up alongside me and they have drums. The song and the beat of the drums all around and the beat of the drums like bare feet hitting packed and moist dirt. Brown yellow golden black people marching and a body wrapped in cloth carried high over the heads of the men. I fall into the marching, my feet taking me wherever they are going. I'm looking up at the body held high over heads like some kind of bridge between sky and earth and a yellow hand, dull with death, is escaping from tightly wrapped cotton. I know that hand, know the simple gold ring on the marriage finger, yellow skin sinking into itself making hands stiff and mummylike.

"Daddy's hand hanging limply from the tightly wrapped white cotton and Daddy's body a bridge between sky and Earth. We are taking Daddy's body to the burial ground. All around me people are holding things that used to belong to Daddy, things that Daddy maybe still loves. We are walking and stomping to the beat of the drums, drums neither fast nor slow but somewhere in between and it isn't any kind of effort for me to keep rhythm or pace. The only time I can ever remember when I'm not falling behind.

"The burial ground is nothing more than a small green field in the middle of a dark and cool forest, just a little sunlight shining through the spaces between branches, reflecting off of bright green leaves. We all stop at the edge of the clearing and ask the spirits for permission to enter. The clearing is quiet and still, no birds and no animals and not even wind moving through the grass and branches. We wait for a long minute, Daddy's body held high over heads, Daddy's lone hand hanging limp and loose from the rest of him and pointing us forward. I miss the signal of the spirits, don't know what to look for, and we all move forward into the clearing. Men digging deep in the dark earth, making a space in all that darkness for Daddy and putting him in the earth just like they put him in the earth when I was a little girl. Me, Mama, Violet, and Rose standing at the side of the grave and wondering where Daddy was because he couldn't be just gone.

"People leaving things that Daddy used to love beside the grave, on top of soft earth rounded like a woman's hips. Daddy's pipe and Daddy's brush and pictures of all of us, all of his girls, and Daddy's favorite tie and Daddy's favorite pair of shoes. I'm standing there with all these people and trying to see Daddy's face, trying to remember and nothing there but his limp and wrinkled old hand. I need pictures and more than the pictures that I have from when I was a little girl. I feel this great wave of panic and loss moving through me and there is nothing for me to hold on to. I just stand there empty-handed and think about all the people I knew and loved, all the heroes gone and nothing at all to mark their passing. Nothing at all that says this was a good person, this person died a horrible death for me and you."

Imani sat quietly, a good distance away from Aunt Lilly, staring at her face, smelling the garden that she kept hidden just beneath her dress and cultivated in her hair, fear and confusion crawling in her belly. She moved farther away from Aunt Lilly, making her way to the door and relieved that Grandma was downstairs. "But why, Aunt Lilly? What does it all mean?"

Aunt Lilly smiled at her; smiled so that her face widened and her eyes almost disappeared.

"It means, darling mine," Aunt Lilly said, "that I have to keep hanging pictures until all the walls and ceilings in the world are covered."

Studio Time

THE MASKLIKE FACE OF A WOMAN lay cracked and jagged on her workbench. Dark brown wood carelessly knocked to the floor by her hands. The expression distorted, the nose completely gone, and eyes that were nothing more than holes, eyes that held no light at all. No light at all and outside the sun was hiding, chased away by gray clouds and damp, cold air and there was steam on the window glass. Early winter and any day she was expecting and dreading snow, how was she going to get around, move, think with her world covered and blanketed and confined to her house?

She stared down at the cracked and broken mask on her floor. Sharp edges where nose and mouth once were, wood so splintered and dangerous that she had to be careful not to prick the firm and worn skin of her palms. She wondered over the how and the why, considered her obvious distraction over Taji and the gentle or fierce persuasiveness of touch, his touch. Loved, blinded by his radiance and women in shards, shattered.

She tried to visualize how to put pieces back together so that it would be a perfect fit. She usually wasn't careless in her studio. She usually knew just what her hands were doing; there wasn't this chasm between thought and act like a bridge down between hand and mind. She picked up the mask, placed the jagged edges together. The mask almost looked whole, like it had never been broken but there was this harsh line, a scar that marred the absolute smoothness of the wood. There was no way that she could glue or re-sculpt or refigure, the break was too harsh, too complete. She placed the pieces of the mask in her lap, dropped her head upon her workbench, and cried.

When she was pregnant with Imani, living on South Street with Charles, her body was battered by tension as things fell apart. Stomach constantly rolling, eyes always tearful and red, long strands of hair in the bathroom sink, skin rashes and eruptions. For nine full months she couldn't breath easy, couldn't take a deep breath until after Imani was born and she had a new reason for living.

She was a lover of women, a creator of women, a daughter, a sister, a mother, and too much of her time was spent trying to figure out men. There was something she wasn't getting, something that she was overlooking—maybe the movement of hands and hips, or the growth of beard and mustache—that left men drifting in the parameters of her world.

And all the time men drawing her in and keeping her still with the fierce tenderness of skin to skin and the confusion of manhood. Keeping her still until the first disappointment, the first intentional hurt. She never saw it coming, certainly not on South Street. She never knew who Charles was angry with, although he said that it was her, everything, all of it her. She sat on the bathroom floor, door locked, listening to him scream and then plead and then scream, she listened to him rant and rave and watched as things fell apart around her. The house always dirty and her hair never combed and no energy to sit quietly and think or work frantically and create, no energy because he was sucking her in. The weaker she became the more abusive he got, an occasional slap across the face, nothing that hurt physically but still left her sobbing and dazed. She found out she was pregnant, didn't know who she was, and knew that she wasn't going to let some strange woman raise her child. She called her mother and sisters to take her home. They came, tight-lipped and closemouthed and relieved because she was breaking free from whatever shit he had her under.

After that she thought that she knew what to look for, knew the signs that were like warnings and hinted that a loss of something precious might be involved. She wasn't prepared for Taji, didn't see him coming and suddenly she was somewhere else, inside of his woman's eyes and everything changed. Guarding herself not from screams and demands and open palms connecting with her cheek; guarding herself from his kindness, his compassion, the way he was with her child, the way he held her at night and let her go in the mornings. She could not work, her woman in shards on her lap, and the thought of misplacing something invaluable hounding her.

Imani

THE SNOW WAS SO DEEP that the stoops were covered and houses looked like they had no steps, like you had to jump from ground to door and hope for the best. Imani wondered how in the world she and Mommy were going to get out of the house if the snow was so deep that there weren't any steps and houses looked like they were floating.

She inhaled deeply, letting her chest fill and abruptly deflate, trying to see if maybe Mommy was up and cooking breakfast. Fresh fruit like grapes and oranges and grapefruits and pears and kiwi and fresh bread straight from the oven or maybe waffles or pancakes spread with apple butter or raspberry jelly.

The house was quiet and still and she went to her bedroom door and cautiously opened it. Mommy's bedroom door was still closed and that meant that Mommy was still sleeping and wasn't even about to get up. Mommy and Taji sleeping and Imani trying to get used to Mommy and Taji and them talking to each other instead of always and all the time talking to her. She went to the bathroom first, and went to the toilet. After she was done she washed her hands and put on a little of Mommy's blush and lip gloss because they were just lying there on the sink and she liked the way lip gloss made her lips look shiny and wet and the blush made her look like she had high cheekbones like Mommy.

She rummaged through the chest of drawers beneath the sink. In the very bottom drawer Mommy kept her tampons and maxi pads. Imani pulled a pad out of its box, rubbed her fingers against the plush, soft surface. She wanted to bleed each month the way that Mommy bled. She wanted to wear the soft pad between her legs and look down into the toilet and see the red from her insides.

Imani placed the pad carefully back in its box, left the bathroom, and walked down the hall to Mommy's studio. The door was closed firmly and Imani opened it and stepped into a world that was so bright because of the morning sun reflecting off the snow that she was almost blinded but still knew and saw that all the faces of the women in the room looked like her. They were all her face or her face how it could have been or maybe would be later when she was no longer a little girl. She closed the door behind her, heard the soft click as the lock fell into place and then there was nothing but silence, nothing but stillness and light all around her and the gentle collective breath of the women, Mommy's women. Some of the women solemn and some laughing and some holding their sides or hearts from pain and some with arms reaching out to hold others. The faces so smooth and elegant, the wood ranging from the deepest ebony to a polished, gleaming brown and mouths full or thin and cheekbones high or round.

She stood still, staring at Mommy's women and as she stood there she heard muffled sounds of distress coming from somewhere in the room. Sounds of distress like the sounds sometimes in her head when she thought about her father and Mommy and Taji and Taji maybe leaving because he wasn't just hers anymore. She turned slowly on her heels, trying to place it and hoping that it was one of Mommy's women trying to get her attention, trying to be her friend, wanting to play with her the way that she played with her girlfriends, Tasha and Marty, outside after school or on Saturday mornings. Outside in the sun and the cold they played house and mommy and school and did dolls' hair and went to work and came home and cooked and put children to bed and went out some nights to rip through the town. She and Tasha and Marty playing grown-up and when she came in the house Mommy waiting and telling her, "Darling mine, you all out there practicing for a role that you don't even have to fill. Not if you don't want to, not before taking a good look around and seeing what else is out there for you."

The sounds of distress were coming from the darkest corner of the room, coming from the giant wastebasket that Mommy put discarded pieces of wood and stone into. Imani went to the wastebasket and stood there peering in. She didn't see anything, couldn't distinguish between the glow of wood and the dull elegance of stone. She saw something that looked like half a face; a woman's face cracked and jagged and she looked in the wastebasket and around the room for blood, a woman's blood. The sounds of distress came from the cracked half of a woman's face and Imani frantically began searching for the other piece. At the very bottom of the wastebasket Imani found the missing piece, the other side, and she gently placed the two sides on the floor and sat down cross-legged. The wood was dark, deep dark and the break was almost right down the middle of the face so that there was no nose really on either piece and each piece had half of a mouth and one eye.

Imani had never seen this woman before and she wondered when Mommy had started working on her and how she got broken in two and how she ended up in the wastebasket crying out her distress. The woman was silent now, staring up at her or trying to through two eyes that were now separate and couldn't work in tandem, trying to smile at her through half a mouth. Imani ran her hands along the crack, caught a small splinter, and pulled her hand away abruptly. Beneath the splinter blood was swelling and Imani pulled the wood out of her index finger with her teeth, spit it out, and sucked at her flesh, her blood sweet against her tongue. What was one of Mommy's women doing in the trash? Imani was horrified by the thought because if Mommy could put one of her women in the trash, if one of her women could end up broken and vulnerable what else could be shattered and discarded?

Imani picked up the two halves of wood, stood and cradled them with one hand against her chest. In her bedroom, she placed the pieces of the woman together and tied yarn around and around like a bandage and knotted it tightly. She placed the woman on the ledge of her windowsill, face pressing against the glass so that she could look out into a world that was large and bright with sun and bright with people and not be reminded of the smallness and darkness of the wastebasket in Mommy's studio.

Imani knew that she was going to be a woman, if not soon then someday, and then what would she do? Being a woman and grown and no one to hold her and no one to kiss away hurts or wipe at runny noses had her scurrying from her room, because of the panic riding in her chest, and knocking on Mommy's closed bedroom door.

"Baby, come in," Mommy said and her voice was drunk from sleep and lazy with happiness.

Imani opened the door and Mommy was in bed with Taji, in bed and sitting up and holding out her arms to her and Taji was still sleeping, his arms around Mommy's waist. Taji and Mommy and sounds of distress in her head and she hoped that Taji didn't leave, like all the men coming and going eventually left. She ran to the bed and crawled into Mommy's arms, Mommy kissed her hair, shifted until they were lying spoon fashion and she was curled into Mommy's warmth, her back cushioned by Mommy's soft belly and round breasts. She breathed them in, Mommy's scent, and Taji's scent, and the way that the room smelled of both of them, of all three of them, but of Mommy the most. The panic in her breast quieted as she lay there underneath the covers, burrowing closer to Mommy's heat and listening to Taji's light snoring. The curtains were pulled closed in the room and shadows played along the floors and ceiling. She watched them for as long as she could, until her eyes became heavy and tired. She drifted, fading in and out because someday she was going to be a woman, wanted to be a woman, but for right now, in this moment, she was just a little girl.

Taji's hair in her face woke her up, hair so heavy and soft and long and dark like all the darkness that ever was at the root and blond at the very ends. Mommy was gone and she could smell French toast or waffles or pancakes from downstairs in the kitchen and she wondered how long she was asleep because all the shadows that had been playing across the ceiling and floors were all in different places, scattered haphazardly about the room. Taji was still softly snoring and he was all sprawled out and taking up all of the space in the bed. She pulled his hair, not really hard, just enough to get his attention and he opened his eyes abruptly and sat straight up.

She laughed at him. "You take up all the room, Taji."

Taji wiped a hand down across his face, and finally smiled. "Was that you pulling on my hair like that?" he asked, trying to put mean in his voice and failing and, anyhow, she knew he wouldn't hurt her.

"You take up all the room," she repeated.

He was still for a moment as if considering. "Yeah, I guess you right. I'm sorry about that. But you hurt my head real bad when you pulled on my hair like that." He was looking pitiful and like his feelings were really hurt.

She scooted up to him, stood on the bed so she could reach the top of his head, and kissed the general spot on his head where she had pulled. She plopped back down and into his lap. "Is that better?"

He hugged her real tight and his hug was different from Mommy's because he didn't have Mommy's softness but it was still nice. "That's much, much better, baby." Then he squeezed her until she was laughing and squealing.

She didn't mind his lap or his smell and his arms were light and sure around her. She had all these pictures in her head, pictures of men almost as dark as Taji but not quite and men as light brown as she was or as yellow as Aunt Lilly or a deep brown like Mommy. Men with hair cut close to the scalp, with huge Afros, long locks or no hair at all. Men with beards and mustaches and glasses and gleaming white teeth. All of them maybe pictures of the father that she had never seen and didn't know who lived behind the laughter or sadness in her eyes. All those pictures fading and shifting and falling to pieces until only Taji's picture remained, he was the only one that she could see clearly.

"It's snowing," Taji said. "Did you see?"

Imani nodded her head against his chest. "When I got up this morning I looked out the window and there was all this snow and I knew that there was no school. You got to go to work?"

"I don't see why I should go to work when you have no school. And anyway, your mommy's downstairs fixing breakfast and I'm hungry, how about you?"

"Yeah, I'm hungry. Are you going to stay here all day, then?"

"I was planning to. Is that all right with you?"

"Uh-huh."

"Okay, let's stop being lazy and get out this bed and see what's for breakfast."

Downstairs Mommy was in the kitchen with the radio on and Curtis Mayfield was singing "It's All Right" and there was snow beneath the window ledge outside and their small backyard was no longer their backyard but some other place altogether, there was no color at all, just blinding whiteness and light. Mommy was making peanut-butter and banana pancakes and Imani almost jumped up and down because peanut-butter pancakes were her favorite.

Taji put a finger to his lips, went to Mommy from behind, put his arms around her, and kissed her quickly on the back of the neck. Mommy jumped but only for show because she knew that they were there.

"Hey, baby. Did you have a bad dream or something last night?" Mommy asked.

"No, I just woke up real early and wanted to come and lay down with you." Imani wanted to ask about the cracked and jagged woman but not now, not when breakfast was cooking and Mommy was smiling and Taji was here.

"Okay, baby. Okay," Mommy said and kissed her. "Let me finish breakfast."

"You need help?" Taji asked, already at the sink and washing dirty dishes.

"You can cut up some fruit when you're done with the dishes."

"Can I help, Mommy?"

"Of course you can." Mommy went to the refrigerator and dug out five large, colorful oranges. "You can peel these so Taji won't have to do it when he cuts up fruit."

They worked in the bright, late morning sun reflecting from off the snow outside and Curtis Mayfield was no longer

201

on the radio; instead it was the Supremes singing "Reflections."

The phone on the wall rang and Mommy turned down the fire under the pancakes and went to answer it. "Hello? Hi, Mama. Nope, she and Taji are right here. We in the kitchen cooking breakfast since there was no school today because of the snow."

Mommy went almost pale and slumped against the kitchen wall.

"What you saying, Mama? Just like that, out of the blue?"

Taji turned down the radio, took the pancakes off the fire, and turned off the stove, went to Mommy and put his arms around her. She leaned against him and all of a sudden she looked very young and very tired and Imani didn't bother with peeling any more oranges.

"What did you say? Oh, God. Oh, God. Mama, what am I going to do, how am I supposed to go back there again? I don't think I can."

Mommy was almost crying and Taji was frowning behind her, his arms tightening around her shoulder and waist and Imani stared down at the table, at the peelings and the lush, ripe flesh of the orange.

"There's a number? I don't know if I want it. I have to think. Let me go now and I'll call you back later. Yeah, I'll be okay. I just don't know why after all this time and what do I say, Mama? What can I possibly say? I know, I know. I love you, too."

Mommy hung up the phone and took deep long breaths.

"What's wrong? What's happened?" Taji asked.

Mommy just shook her head. "Imani, I need you to go

upstairs for a minute so that Taji and I can talk. Can you do that for me?"

Imani didn't want to go, she knew a grown-up discussion was about to take place and she wanted to hear what grown-ups talked about when children weren't around and she wanted to know what had upset Mommy so much.

"Okay." She hopped off the chair, and left the kitchen, feet dragging. She was as far as the living room when she heard Mommy break down, it wasn't crying, it was deeper than crying, more like wailing, and the sound held Imani still, her hand on the railing leading up the stairs.

She heard Taji say, "Baby, tell me what's wrong. It can't be as bad as this. Please, tell me what's wrong."

Mommy said, "Imani's father called Mama. He wants to see her after all this time and I've never told her anything about him, nothing, because I was trying to forget."

Imani's hand fell from the railing, her knees buckled beneath her, she dropped to the floor and placed her thumb in her mouth—something she hadn't done since she was four years old. Her father calling and altering all of the pictures that she had been carving and shaping for Taji. Her father was never so real and she didn't understand why Mommy was crying, what did this man do that the very mention of his name made Mommy break down and be someone else, vulnerable and unrecognizable? And who was she if her father was not hiding behind her sometimes laughing and sometimes crying eyes and actually out there in the world and for all this time, her whole life, wanting no part of her?

Studio Time

THE SNOW MELTING, dripping from the roof and window ledges, snow melting and falling like tears to the wet and soggy ground. She watched from her studio table, watched patiently as each water droplet formed and then fell, a cycle that repeated itself over and over. There was nothing in front of her, no pencils or charcoal or sketches or pieces of wood or slabs of stone. Her hands were spread out on her worktable, fingers separated and curled, rough palms resting against the dark gray surface like she was old, so old, and her hands and fingers just needed a break from constant action.

The women were silent today, overwhelmed and sympathetic in the face of her absolute confusion. Women staring at her with nothing but compassion because they knew what it meant to be in between a rock and hard place with no inkling of how to do the right thing or even if there was a right thing to do. Her little woman child watching her with wounded eyes, because somehow she knew, and all the breath leaving her body, escaping in quiet, desperate pants because her child was never supposed to hurt like this. She didn't know how to gather up the falling pieces and put them back together for her. She couldn't make herself say, "Yes, I left him because he hurt me in the end. He really hurt me and I never saw it coming, not at all. And no, he didn't want you but I did. I have always wanted you and I always will." She had never been able to get those words out, not when Imani was four and had noticed that other children had fathers and all she had was a mother, so she had said nothing at all and in saying nothing had left her child licking at wounds that she wasn't sure that she could make better.

And her saying, "He didn't want you," to her eight-year-old child and watching her face crumple and cave in on itself and her mouth struggle to form a question that there really wasn't any answer to was just the beginning. She didn't even have the words to say the rest, and even if there were words she couldn't get them out of the throat, couldn't watch her child's eyes accuse and worry and wonder over how come why now and what does this mean and what does this make me?

The why and the how and the who all had to do with the when and she didn't want to go back to that when because there was nothing there but heartache. They were so young, everyone young, even the old, that they forgot all about caution, forgot all about disappointment.

In the end everyone dead and nothing and no one changed. She couldn't even change herself, couldn't forget where Mama came from or how Lilly was getting high or why Violet's highest goal in life was to be a lady or why she was pregnant and hiding under tables and in closets. She couldn't change Imani's father, couldn't get inside and re-arrange the basic pattern of who he was and who he was going to turn out to be. She couldn't stop him from catego-rizing her body parts or using slurs for endearments or taking her pain and calling it pleasure and so she left and he was happy to see her go, happy to go back to what his life was supposed to be before everyone got caught up in love and revolution.

She studied her hands on the table, studied the long fin-gers that were curled under and the scars on the back of her hands, tiny tattoos decorating her dark brown skin. Her nails were short and blunt, unpolished. The skin of her hands was firm and tough and smooth, no underlying softness at all. Her life was in her hands, in the images that her hands imag-ined and then brought to life. When she was a little girl Mama used to tell her that all thought originated in the mind, that the mind was the most important thing. She knew better, knew that the best part of her was centered in her hands, in the slim, small fingers and the callused palms and short and blunt fingernails. The best part of her day in and day out moving with care and patience over wood and stone, listening to inanimate objects that were alive and si-lence and her history and her womb and her hands capturing it all with skill and precision. Her hands holding her child, hands strong and capable and hands that could put food on the table and hands that could provide because they had to. The best part of her in her hands and child and her hands couldn't move and her child was wounded.

Taji

H E KNEW ROSE HAD A PAST, knew that she wasn't just born when he met them, she was doing all kinds of things for all kinds of reasons long before there ever was an "us" or a "we" and nothing he could hold against her or take away or try to change because it was done. All done and Taji all the time wondering how. She never mentioned it, never opened her mouth to say, "And by the way . . ."

That's all he wanted.

Something like that shouldn't be left unsaid because when it comes out, when some motherfucker calls talking about what he wants and what's best for a child he's never even seen, nothing to do but act like a fool in her house, try not to think about him fucking her.

The person she was now having everything to do with where she had been and who she had been with and he knew that, knew all about forgetting places and not mentioning things, large parts of his life edited, only told what he could stomach telling and why should she or anyone else be any different? Knew all that and knew that she was waiting on trust and waiting on time and waiting to see but something like that, something that made him see different and feel different shouldn't have been left unsaid.

Loving her and being up under and watching her work and thinking that she was his. His to love and to hold and to get inside and now nothing holding them together except for what was unsaid.

On his early morning jog, jogging through narrow streets, past row houses, children heading for school and staring and laughing at him. Air moving fast through his body with blood and flesh wet with sweat, lungs and chest expanded. Running and running and running and trying not to think about her, trying not to feel the hurt that was curled up beneath his balls and the anger gathered like tears at the corners of his eyes.

Beneath his balls hurt, beneath his balls where her hands and fingers and mouth had been, beneath his balls warm, private, defenseless space and he had lain still for her on her sheets smelling of rose and lavender and them, lain still for her eyes closed and vulnerable like he tried not to be vulnerable all the time with anyone else. Her hands and fingers and mouth beneath his balls and moving up into him, up through bowels and intestines and stomach and kidneys and lungs to grab for his heart.

He had lain still. And now thinking that maybe he should have moved, took hands and fingers and mouth off of him because she was inside him now and no way to get her out and she wasn't who he thought she was. Stranger woman, woman he really didn't know anything about, stranger woman moving around in his insides and making him squirm and want and hurt.

Jogging and coming up on Fairmount Park, being overtaken by dry brown grass and bare trees and gray and overcast open sky. Sidestepping melting snow and puddles of ice, canvas sneakers getting wet and wet seeping through socks to reach bare feet. Breath heaving from his mouth like steam or fog, mouth open, jaw loose and slack. He counted his breaths, counted his breaths and tried to feel his body, be in his body and shut down everything else but legs eating up road and swinging arms and motion, totally in the moment. She kept pulling him back to her, pulling him back to her with her face two mornings ago when her mama called, called and just that easy everything he saw himself having with her changed and made into something else. Watching her face on the phone with her mama and watching her face drain of him and Imani and waking up snowed in and loved and safe, because that's what they were before that phone call—safe.

Her face empty and her body slumped against the bright yellow kitchen wall and Imani sitting at the kitchen table wide-eyed and still and the only thing he could do was to go to her and put his arms around her waist and lips at her neck and ask. Ask and wait because whatever she said was fine, whatever she said he could help her carry.

She sent Imani upstairs and just the two of them left in the room. The fire on the stove was turned off and breakfast completely forgotten and fresh fruit going soft in the open air on the table. The yellow walls of the kitchen sucking her in, stealing all her color and she looked dull and washed out and limp and flat.

He waited and waited and nothing came from her and he said, "Tell me what's wrong, baby. Just tell me."

She looked up at him, seeing something else somewhere else where he couldn't go, a place where he couldn't reach and right then at that moment he felt the first brush of hurt beneath his balls. "Charles called Mama. After all this time he wants to see Imani."

"Charles is her father?" He had never asked, never asked for names or reasons because nothing she could say would have any effect on where and what they were now, what he wanted to have with her.

"If you want to call him that, yes."

Her eyes were hard and brittle and scarred and he wanted to rub the fear from her skin, kiss away the pain. "First time in how long since you heard from him?" The entire time sleeping in her bed and holding her at night and trying to really know her Imani's father never mentioned, no names and no stories. Imani was Rose's and no one else's. Imani, the child who he loved long before he started following Rose through the streets. Imani's father was not important and it was just easier to act like she had no father because he wanted them, he wanted them and a new life, he wanted to forget where and who he had been. With them the killer and almost addict was gone and he was just a lover and a father.

"Since before Imani was born. Since I was eighteen and pregnant and trying to figure out how I was going to raise a child when I was with this man who made me not like who I was and where I came from and how I saw things, this man who hurt me, Taji."

He didn't want to hear this, having her say it and the first time realizing that there were things he didn't want to know, things about her that would make her less herself and less his and he didn't want to know but they were here at this moment and there was no way to go back. "Can you tell me what happened, Rose? Do you want to tell me what happened?"

She told him and with every word she said something else about her became different, something else about her not true and not what he thought and not what he wanted and the hurt spreading like spilled water beneath his balls, making his balls ache and sweat and anger clenching teeth and fingers and toes. Angry that some man had put his hands on her, angry that some man had made her feel less than what and who she was, angry that some man yelled at her behind locked doors.

Angry with her because she stayed. Angry at her because she was there in the first place. There in the first place and people dead and earth not even settled, graves not even dug yet all throughout the South, cities up North going up in flames and rage and her falling into free love and easy answers like simple sex was a remedy for death and murder, hatred and contempt.

Angry with her and when she was quiet, when there were no more words and she was still leaning against the kitchen wall, still being sucked in and washed out by the bright yellow tiles the first thing out of his mouth, the very first thing, was, "How could you? How could you?" How could she have gotten around or overlooked or rationalized who she was and who he was and what that meant? Like all she had to do was think differently or see differently and like magic everything would change just because she wanted or needed it to. People gone crazy, running from one end of the country to the other, practicing free love and getting high, too crazy to realize love was never free and who you lay down with, who you let inside you meant something, not meant to be blind or faked pleasure. She, stranger woman he loved, sucked in by the chaos and the optimism and love nothing more than opening legs and closing eyes and hoping for the best.

He rested a minute, leaned against the damp bark of a huge tree, socks almost totally wet and face frozen with cold, and thought about her face, her face fading into the yellow wall and her eyes watching him and bleeding because "How could you?" leaving her vulnerable and open and hurt and something between them precious gone and he wanted explanations and answers and she became smaller and smaller, curled into herself.

He didn't want to touch her because thinking about him touching her, thinking about her lying still for him, and kissing him, and putting her arms around him caused hurt to explode beneath his balls, explode and leave fire in his throat and eyes and he said, pushing her further into the yellow wall, "Damn it, Rose. Damn it."

She was quiet, waiting for it all to come out and no way for him to stop and his voice getting harder and harder.

"How could you have never said shit about it? Why? What were you thinking?"

Hardness in his voice pulling her back into herself, and she stood straight, the yellow wall fading behind her. "How could I have never said shit about what, Taji? My life before you was just that. My life. I don't need to justify anything to anyone. And if you think you need answers, if you think that you can't deal with who I was then, you should leave. As a matter of fact, leave right now. I can't deal with you and this and how to tell Imani all at the same time. I can't."

He went upstairs got dressed and left and that was two days ago and he hadn't been back. He pushed himself away from the tree and headed home, moving at a slower pace, cooling down. His body strong and slim and two days and he missed her touch, two days and he just missed her.

Studio Time

ALL THE TIME TELLING STORIES, stories about purple-black and brown and red and yellow and almost white women, all the time shaping lives and histories and bodies and faces that all had some kind of beginning, middle, and end. None of it not true, all of it bits of the truth, all of it a little bit of the story about what it means to be purple-black and yellow and brown and red and almost white in the United States or anywhere else where being any or all of those things sometimes the same as being fucked over and fucked up and just and simply fucked.

Telling stories but not her story, because she was brown and woman and she had been fucked up and fucked over and fucked and she had no words for any of it. No words because saying it aloud would make it more true. More true, and more true meant everything to do with who she was, and who she was was something different and unexpected if her story allowed space in the fabric of her life and not pushed to corners and closets, forgotten or retold because easier and none of it was.

Taji holding her and loving her and making plans and talking future and all of that changed, maybe gone because making herself up not good enough for him, making herself up and it came out anyway.

Taji making her into everything that he ever wanted "black" and "woman" to mean and be and overlooking and ignoring everything about her that didn't fit into whatever it was he needed, whatever he was prepared to love. She was making herself over for Imani and herself and Taji and any other black male so-and-so and black male somebody grounded in black politics and looking to be held.

Black woman and artist and mother and lover of black men and black people and black community and the story that she couldn't tell, her story changing all that, changing everything. Making Taji's wide, wet woman's eyes go hard and brittle and mean, making space between them where there was none, hurt between them where there was none.

She didn't owe him explanations. Thinking about him sitting at her kitchen table, about to eat her food, playing with her child, just leaving her bed and body and demanding explanations. His face not a face she recognized and his voice making her small, making her hide against walls, inside herself.

She told him to leave and he left, just like that. Left without kisses and smiling eyes and words. Just left. Didn't know if he was coming back or when but she was waiting on him, waiting on him because her story untold leaving her in fragments and leaving Imani in fragments and there were things she wanted to tell Taji. Things about being eighteen years old and black and woman and things about men touching and silencing and reshaping and renaming, things about love and what she thought was love and how sometimes love started off as novelty and ended in contempt.

Lilly

VIOLET WAS COMING HOME and Mama was relieved and Lilly just sat and waited, waited on the couch in the living room trying to keep herself as small and as still as possible. Mama walked around her and over her and would have walked straight through her if she were standing up.

She hoped Violet brought magazines with her, she was running out of magazines. She didn't have anything new, nothing to look through for pictures of faces like her own with eyes that told the truth and not of some candy world.

Lilly heard the car pull up outside the house. She went to the door with Mama and Violet was climbing out of her new red car and all her stuff was piled in the front and back seats like she was carting treasure to a secret hideaway. Violet looking long and lean and her face clear, for the first time in months or maybe years, of worry and frustration and her dark skin smooth and unlined like a child's. Her permed straight, flying hair all gone, cut off at the root and nothing left but tight curls lying soft against her head and high fore-head and huge eyes.

Violet was never the beautiful one, always too stiff and too serious and too harsh and too damn coy like she was practicing for the role of Southern Belle in some Tennessee Williams play. Violet always kept hidden behind makeup and glitter and batting eyelashes and childlike tantrums that were frightening. Violet walking around with her head held high and her Southern Belle hair flying and speaking in soft tones when she really wanted to yell, to hurt, to kill.

"Hey!" Violet called from the car, motioning to them. Lilly grabbed her coat and hat from the closet and went out to help her unload the car.

Mama said, "Tell Violet I'm in the kitchen making tea and slicing carrot cake when you all get done." Mama treating her like she had already overdosed somewhere in an abandoned house or alleyway and was lying cold in the grave.

Violet looked at her long and hard as she came out the front door and skipped down the steps. Lilly knew what she was thinking, knew what they all were thinking but she smiled, feeling her lips strain against her teeth and her tongue swelled and become awkward in her mouth. Violet hugged her hard and she smelled of too-sweet perfume and musk and coconut hair oil.

Violet ran her hands over the length of Lilly's locks falling from beneath her hat. "Every time I see you, you seem to get smaller and smaller."

Lilly felt her lips stretch over her teeth even more. "I like your hair." She touched Violet's soft, tight curls. "You look like you now."

Violet laughed. "Who did I look like before?"

Lilly just stared at her, at the dark skin, the full mouth, the high forehead and cheekbones. "I don't know. I could never really figure it out. You just always looked like someone else."

Violet laughed but her eyes were sad as she thought it through. "Lilly, I guess that makes us even because you've been walking around looking like someone else for a long time, too."

Lilly's lips couldn't stretch anymore and her teeth and jaw actually hurt. "How are the boys doing? They take it okay?"

"They took it fine. They wanted to stay with their father and they're almost grown and I didn't want them. Horrible thing to say, right? I didn't want them with me and, anyway, they didn't need me."

She was sorry for Violet. Jerome was something that Violet had always wanted, since they had started dating in high school. Violet had worked in a department store for a while, selling cosmetics and perfume, but she stopped working after the first baby and all of a sudden her whole life her man and her kids and she was absolutely lost. Violet was in need of a search party, a path, a light to find her way back to herself without the distraction of husband and kids or the detour of ladylike.

Violet reached out and with her long fingers eased the smile from Lilly's lips, kissed her full mouth like she used to when they were younger and Mama was working and Lilly sitting in her lap and feeling safe because Violet loved her enough and was mean enough to keep all the bad things away.

The hurting of jaw and teeth dissolved with the forced smile and Lilly walked easily into Violet's arms. "I love you. I always have."

Violet held tight and Lilly's fragile bones began to break and crumble. "I know. Lilly, I know. I love you. I always have."

This was a funeral rite, a last good-bye, and Lilly couldn't figure out who was given the final kiss, who was going into the ground. Funeral marching and Mama's house and street and sidewalk and Violet's almost new car fading or forming a procession line. It was too much, standing with Violet and all her hair cut off and the search party successful in finding her sister who she assumed was missing in action all of these years, kissing good-bye and hello.

"What are we going to do?" Lilly whispered against Violet's skin, wanting to nibble at her neck, to suck at her flesh like a baby groping for mother's milk or a lover trying to swallow flesh.

"We're going to be fine. We have no choice," Violet said and Lilly knew that Violet was just talking bullshit, had regulated her back to crazy high sister because there was nothing but choice. It wasn't that easy, Violet knew it wasn't that easy and Lilly pulled away from her because the moment for funeral rites, for good-byes and hellos and tenderness had passed and she was left with something sour in the mouth and something aching in the breast. Violet standing in front of her puzzled and worried and face crumpling. She wanted the needle, the sharp prick and the slow piercing of skin and vein and the fire fanning out viciously from her center, burning everything until it all seemed easy.

"What's happening with you, Lilly? What you doing to yourself?"

There was this pressure in her head, she lifted her arms and tried to squeeze it out.

"Lilly, I'm coming home now and things will be different. You got to free yourself up, baby. You got to. You got to free yourself up like I left Jerome and cut my hair because you were right—all those years I was someone else." Violet speaking urgently, grabbing at Lilly's clothes, running her hands over Lilly's skin and Lilly just watched her, stunned. What the hell was Violet talking about? All these black and brown and yellow and red people hanging on her bedroom wall with tired faces and empty eyes or faces made harsh with pain and eyes rolling back in the head. Freedom had to be more than cutting or locking the hair or leaving a man, any man. She walked away from her.

"Lilly, don't be like that. Come on in the house. Don't make me and Mama worry over you like that." Lilly looked back and Violet was standing there free with her new hair and almost crying and she wanted to pick up something, maybe a bottle to hit her with.

"I'm not crazy, Violet. I might be a drug addict but I'm sure as hell not the crazy one." She turned the corner, left the house, Violet and Mama behind, and leaned against the wall of a nearby row house. It was so cold and once-white snow piled along the curbs of the sidewalk like mountains of shit. A little girl on her way home from school, pigtails sticking out from beneath her hat, smiling at her and walking around her cautiously like she was going to bend down and swallow her whole.

Lilly watched the little girl walk down the street. There was already a womanly roll to her hips and her body looked round, a woman's shape. All the little girls, even her darling Imani, in a hurry to get tits and ass and grow up like it was some kind of accomplishment and not just simple biology.

The wind was biting into her face, she could feel her color coming up. Mama and Violet inside warm and sitting over tea and carrot cake and probably talking about her because what else, after all, was there for them to talk about? Mama sipping tea and shrugging her shoulders and saying, "I can't worry over that child anymore. She's not going to put me in my grave. None of my children are going to do that." And Violet shaking her head and running her fingers over her short soft curls simply because they felt so good, so different from flying Southern Belle hair, and saying, "But what we going to do, Mama? Something has to be done because she is out there doing God knows what and killing herself. Maybe we could get her in one of those programs . . ." They would go back and forth like that, in the warmth of the kitchen, steam from teacups on their faces and the sweetness of carrot cake coating their tongues. They didn't know that she was all the time fighting, all the time baring her teeth and holding up her fists and standing her ground like a prizefighter. It was just that she had a glass jaw, was quick to hit the mat, the ground, dirt, whatever and no one else really gave two fucks.

The cold of the wall was seeping through her coat, bleeding through wool and cotton to reach her skin, and she shoved herself away and began walking, head down against the wind and gloved hands balled in her pockets. The ground moved quickly beneath her feet, the cement was damp with melting snow and icy with cold. Her booted feet stomping carelessly through shallow puddles and glossy ice.

Her blood was raging now and she could feel it moving slow and thick through her body like molten lava. She wondered why she didn't blow up or melt down and she wanted the needle digging into her flesh and easier, at long last easier. She lifted her head, getting her bearings and began walking to the Corner.

The Corner and men in cars constantly cruising by and it didn't matter if they were old or young or black or white or Latino. They all wanted the same thing, the desire was written around the eyes and the mouth, in the carelessness of their hands against her flesh.

They didn't want gentleness. She wasn't fooled, she knew them, knew them better than wives or mothers or daughters ever could, knew the things they asked her to do. She didn't know that there were so many places on her body that a random man could forcefully shove a hard dick into. She didn't know that her body was nothing more than open and wounded orifices waiting to be filled and all in silence. They didn't care if she cried, buried her face against dirty sheets or pillows or the cool leather of cold car seats; they didn't care if she screamed and went to the bathroom or to the sidewalk to throw up afterward. They paid her or sometimes they didn't pay, they hurt her or sometimes didn't hurt her, and she wasn't any kind of judge at all. She couldn't stare at the face, notice the light or lack of light in the eye or if the shirt was stained and wrinkled and determine whether or not there was danger or safety.

It was cold and the Corner wasn't as crowded as usual but it was crowded enough. Women in stolen or free winter coats and hats and scarves and gloves sitting and walking around waiting for someone to stop. She didn't know any of the women, not really. Women with faces like the brown yellow black and red faces screaming on her wall.

Lilly wondered what women thought about when fingers were in mouths or pussies or asses and women making sounds like really bad porno movies and some man was grunting or swearing or hollering for more or harder or faster or wider like he had bought and paid for all of her and not just the necessary parts.

She walked back and forth on the Corner with caution. Her feet lifted her high above the ground because she had never been able to control the floating of her body when she walked, like gravity had no meaning to her body's center. Rose used to call her angel child, called her that all the time and was constantly drawing her body in motion. A car stopped just in front of her and Lilly wondered if the man behind the wheel stopped because he noticed the way that her feet didn't touch the ground, noticed the way that her locks fell like water from beneath her hat.

Her lips stretched across her teeth in what was almost a smile but not quite because there was something rotten in her mouth, something rotten in her that she couldn't make go away no matter how many times she spit or swallowed or brushed her teeth. The sweet, dense smell of marijuana rolled out of the car in waves and she could hardly see a face through the smoke. He was black, had Mama and Violet's deep dark skin and he was absolutely still watching her. She hated this part, hated the first moment of conversation, getting the terms of the deal hashed out because it was all pointless. He knew—she was sure he knew just by looking at her—that she would do anything at all. Her tongue tripped and stumbled over the words, could only manage a soft and girlish, "Hi, how you doing?"

Clearing smoke revealed his face and his features were fine—mouth wide and long-lashed eyes—and waiting. "Can you get in?"

She hesitated. "I don't do anal. Everything else but not that."

"Okay. Get in." He reached over and unlocked and opened the passenger door and Lilly fumbled her way into the car. The smell of marijuana was all around her and she sucked it into her lungs, let the smoke fill up the rottenness and felt her eyes tear.

He said, "I got a spot not too far from here. Can I take you there?" He didn't smile, just kept watching her and she shifted uncomfortably.

"How far is not too far from here?" Lilly knew all the stories about women being trapped in a remote room for days, weeks, with hands and feet tied to the bed and a piece of cloth shoved in the mouth to muffle the screams.

"Off of Broad and Erie. Like I said, not too far from here."

Broad and Erie was still in her neighborhood. She could

scream for help if she had to and someone would come. "Okay."

"My name's Malik. You got a name?" He smiled and his smile made his solemn, fine face beautiful.

"Lilly. My name's Lilly." She crossed her hands demurely in her lap and studied her blunt and ragged fingernails.

The car stopped and Lilly opened the passenger door and stepped over the snow piled high like shit and waited on him, waited on Malik. He took her arm with just enough force to guide her. He took her inside a house where all the windows were dark and Lilly, despite his smile, felt alarm and tried to keep herself steady. "You live here?" The floors of the house were wooden and rough and didn't have the shine of Mama's floors. The walls were deep, cool shades of green.

"I live here. Me and a few friends." He closed the door behind him and the room was large, larger than the room that she had at Mama's house. He had pictures hanging from the walls, covering all the walls. She recognized the tangled and lush jungle of the Amazon, the beauty of the Ivory Coast, the cool glaciers of the Antarctic, the flat plains of Middle America, and the towering buildings of the inner city.

"I like your pictures," she told him, circling so that she could spend a few moments looking over each.

He shrugged his shoulders. "They're places I haven't been that I want to get to."

"There're so many places to go."

He laughed and his laughter was more nicer than his

smile. "Don't I know. Don't I know." He quieted, stared, and then said, "Take off your hat, let me see all that hair."

Lilly took off the hat, placed her hands at her scalp, and shook out her hair.

He just watched and waited. "You know, I don't think I've ever seen hair like that on anyone up close. I see it on Jamaicans in pictures but never on someone just walking around the streets. That's why I picked you up, because of your hair."

She thought about Violet and her new hair and her new freedom that really wasn't because freedom couldn't be that shallow or that easy. She felt the weight of her locks hanging down her back, shrugged her shoulders. "It's just hair. Nothing much to it at all except to leave it alone and let it grow."

"It's beautiful hair."

She actually blushed, it had been that long since anyone had given her something nice and she wanted to ignore the fire in her blood and the rottenness in her mouth and the reason why she was standing in his room with him, surrounded on all sides by places that neither of them had ever been.

"Do you want to smoke?" he asked.

She was surprised that he offered and grateful for anything that would make the whole thing easier. "Yes. Yes, I want to smoke."

He went to the top drawer of his dresser and pulled out at least a half ounce of marijuana and some rolling paper. He sat on the floor and began rolling joints. She stared. He laughed again. "Weed and women. My only vices."

"I wish I only had two."

"Yeah?" he asked and carefully sprinkled weed onto the white flat-top paper. "How many you got?"

"Too many to count, way too many." She sat down cross-legged on the floor next to him.

He lit the joint, inhaled a couple of times, and passed it to her. The joint was light between her fingers. She used to smoke all the time before she started shooting up and then there was no point to it, marijuana nothing more than a tease. They smoked two joints companionably in silence and he put on some music—Curtis Mayfield—and she was almost comfortable when he said, "Do you want to take off your clothes now?" Said it so politely and respectfully and she was so mellow that she thought maybe he said something else altogether but he was staring at her, just waiting. She floated to her feet and took off her heavy winter coat first. He put the joint in the top of a tin can as the coat fell to the floor in front of him. She unfastened her blue-collared shirt and it slid down her body. She didn't bother with a bra because she was so skinny and never had much on top anyway. She unfastened her jeans and slid them off along with her panties and stepped out of them. She was miserable, her feet floating just above the floor and the weight of her hair hanging down her back and she wanted to cut her head off from her body completely.

He stood and his hands were on her skin and his hands were warm and she wasn't turned off or turned on or scared or anything, she was just tired. She felt his fingers on her inner arm, running over the fragile, baby skin and the harsh blue and purple and deep yellow of her bruises covered with scabs.

"This is what you're doing to yourself?" he asked and she didn't answer, just stood there still under his fingers. "I was trying to figure out why you were out there like that, looking all anxious and confused. I'm not going to hurt you. I won't and I'll pay you, you don't have to worry about that."

He sat her on his bed like she was a doll and she wanted nothing more than to lie down and sleep as she watched him take off his clothes. He was a big man, his limbs long and there was fat at his middle and along his sides and his skin was dark like Mama and Violet's and he had said that he wouldn't hurt her and that was all she wanted at this point, not to be hurt. He sat next to her on the bed and kissed her and his kiss was overpowering and his hands were in her hair, repeatedly tugging and separating the locks, and she let his hands place her head however he liked.

She kept her eyes closed and counted her heartbeats. Her heart beating slowly and erratically so that she couldn't keep a steady count, heart beating like it was slowing down for good and she couldn't imagine anything nicer or anything that made more sense. He paused to get a condom from his dresser, he kept his condoms and his marijuana in the same drawer and for some reason that made her smile. She stared at the pictures on the wall as he fumbled with the condom. She listened to the wrapper being torn open and imagined that she was in the tangled and lush jungle of the Amazon. He came back to the bed and she was wandering through the flat plains of Middle America. When he came she was already swimming in the warm waters of the Ivory Coast. His face was wet against hers, his sweat making her eyes tear and stinging her skin and she didn't mind because he had given just what he had promised. She felt his body stiffen and heard his grunt and it was over. He lay still against her for a moment, careful to balance his weight on his elbows and his hands and face in her hair.

He rolled off of her. "Do you want to sleep?"

She was already gone, had just enough energy to nod her head and pull the sheet to her waist.

She woke, startled, from the dream that she had whenever she closed her eyes. There was smoke in the room and the man with the deep dark skin like Mama and Violet was a deadweight next to her. She couldn't remember his name, just his kindness and that he had offered her rest. The smoke was thick and black and she could smell the fire, knew that the fire all the time raging inside of her had somehow broken through the barrier of blood and flesh. She tried to shake the man next to her, but he didn't move and the smoke was so thick and she was breathing it in and decided to stay where she was.

Studio Time

S HE DIDN'T KNOW how to sketch or sculpt putting a sister into the ground. She felt her hands filled with earth, earth damp and warm and alive, and digging and digging to bury flesh of her flesh but different, always different and no more. Hands filled with earth and mouth full of dust, dry because ashes to ashes and dust to dust, and there was no need or use for tears. Going over to Mama's house to make sense and make plans and to figure out how even though everyone knew that this was coming, maybe not coming this soon or this way but coming. Mama holding her womb like it would fall out between tightly closed thighs and land in a mess between her feet because what was the womb without the child even if the child was a grown woman walking around gibbering baby talk and having fretful baby dreams?

Grown woman with hair locked down the back turned red at the ends by sun and time and bruises and scars lining the tender skin of pale yellow arms and slender hands with nails bitten off and bleeding.

She wanted to get rid of the memories of blood of her blood high and sitting in vomit and shit and piss; get rid of the memory of Lilly begging for money or fucking for money, doing anything to anyone for a hit; and, Lord God, especially get rid of the memory of Lilly burning up in a house not too far from Mama's with some strange man lying next to her.

She wondered what he looked like. Was he red and golden and yellow like Lilly, did he have Imani's brown and shining skin, or was he dark like Violet and Mama and Taji? She knew that he had probably picked Lilly up from a corner somewhere, probably saw her hair hanging and her feet floating like she belonged on a fucking island or in the green country of the South, anywhere but where she was.

Taji could help, had offered help, even though his face still beaten up about where she had been and who she had been with and what that made her. Opening the door the day she found out and Taji standing there and opening his arms and holding her. They didn't talk about what was left unsaid, no time with pain numbing her heart and Lilly waiting to be buried. Thankful he was there, thankful and weary and waiting because nothing between them was resolved and the tension between who she was and what she told him she was and what he wanted her to be was always there.

She didn't know how to let him in, didn't know how to explain to anyone what Lilly was to her. Her first real love and her first real heartbreak. Looking at her and all the time touching her shoulder or hands or face—her fingertips tracing Lilly's shy smile and open, vulnerable eyes. Looking at her and looking at her until looking wasn't enough and she had to draw her. Draw Lilly writing poetry or Lilly singing gospel or Lilly swaying with Billie Holiday and hopping up and down with the Temptations.

Paper and pencil or charcoal and pencil could not capture all the dimensions of Lilly's facial expressions, could only hint at the length and fragility of her limbs, the beauty of her body in motion, the way she smiled not just with mouth and eyes but with her whole body. She hunted deserted and unused pieces of wood and stone and began to sculpt.

She tried the face first because it was the face that she loved best of all and it seemed the easiest place to begin. It took her months to learn to be gentle enough with the chisel to get the outline of Lilly's eyes just right, took her an entire year until she was satisfied that she had gotten the entire face to almost look like Lilly. There was still something missing, something that the eye couldn't see but the heart felt that she knew would take her years to get just right.

She had forgotten about all that, forgotten about why she started sculpting and the art that Lilly had given her. Still, all her women looked liked her sister, all of them had parts of Lilly and some of them were even the whole of Lilly and she wondered if she had ever loved anyone else that consistently or intensely other than her child. Her first love and her first heartbreak her golden and red and yellow sister with hair down the back and sad eyes being put into the ground.

Rose

PICTURES OF BLACK AND RED AND YELLOW AND brown people screaming on Lilly's wall, pictures that had to come down because there was no way that those pictures were going to be any kind of memorial, no way that they were going to allow those pictures to say anything the slightest bit significant about Lilly and what Lilly wanted and what Lilly needed.

The funeral in four days' time and Lilly's body burned and blackened. They were going to have a closed casket because there was no more Lilly, no body, just a burnt dead thing. Nothing left of Lilly but dental records and the small silver pendant of a flower that Mama had given them all when they turned sixteen.

Mama dressed in sweatpants and T-shirt, Violet in ragged jeans and tank top, Imani sitting on the front stoop dressed in a purple jumpsuit, like a little girl even though Rose knew she was moving further and further away from talking to dolls and little-girl dreams.

Mama said, "Okay, here are trash bags and I already took the ladder up so that we can reach the pictures on the ceiling. Clothes in one trash bag for the Salvation Army, things we want to keep in another trash bag, and all those magazine pictures on the walls and things we want to throw away in another trash bag."

"Is there anything in particular you want to keep, Mama?" Violet asked.

"I can't think of anything off the top of my head, but we'll see once we get up there and get started. Rose, you ready?"

"I'm ready, Mama," she said but she was tired and all Mama's planning was not going to make the whole thing easier.

The climb up the stairs was steep and dangerous, at every step Rose was assaulted by a memory of Lilly. First step and seeing Lilly jump rope, second step and watching Lilly dance to Billie Holiday, third step and hearing Lilly sing gospel, hear Lilly belting out Mahalia Jackson, fourth step and rubbing Lilly's back when her period came on and she had cramps, fifth step and making Lilly sit still for her so that she could sketch her and on and on it went until she reached the top of the stairs. Top of the stairs and vision blurred and she was so weak that she had to lean against Violet.

"All right?" Violet asked.

She nodded her head and rubbed a hand against her weeping heart. "Yes. Yes, I'm all right."

Mama marching to Lilly's room and opening the door and just standing there, looking inside.

"Mama?" Rose asked.

Mama shook her head. "Just give me a minute. You all go ahead in and get started. I just need a minute, that's all."

The room was quiet and still and dead like Lilly was dead. Pictures of black and yellow and brown and red people on the wall and Lilly's single bed in the center of the room and Lilly's dolls from childhood on top of the dresser. Violet went to the closet and immediately began to pull and drag out shirts and jeans and shoes and winter coats and fall jackets. A pile of clothes in the center of the room and Mama came in and sat cross-legged on the floor and began sorting, making two separate piles, trash and clothes still in good enough condition for the Salvation Army.

Violet and Mama busy and not looking up or around, not looking at all those pictures on the wall the same way that Rose wanted not to look or touch or tear down but Mama and Violet had left it all to her and she really didn't see any way to get out of it, any way to explain what they all knew—pictures on the wall the very worst part of Lilly and what killed her just as much as needles digging in flesh and smoke and fire. She tore down pictures from around the door first, because they were nearest to her and she wanted to create a safe exit just in case any of them needed to escape.

Door free of pictures and no faces like prison and pain keeping you still with shocked, bleeding eyes. Pictures out of magazines frail and tearing and crumpling easy in her hand, falling like first winter snowflakes into the black plastic trash bag at her feet. Picture of black woman and baby thin and wasted in some place where there was no food; picture of yellow man with face bloodied and hands tied behind the back, and mouth gagged in a place without air or sun or water; picture of red child, motherless, and big bellied from malnutrition and sad; picture of entire brown family standing in their front yard and staring, transfixed, at a burning cross. It was too much, all of it was too much and Rose was trying to put it all together, trying to make sense out of it.

Lilly spending days and nights and weeks huddled in her room, digging through magazines and newspapers and encyclopedias and dictionaries. Pictures used like rose or tulip wallpaper, taped and glued on like starving, crying people were really fashionable and helped to brighten a room. Pieces of plaster peeled off with pictures and falling at her feet and the edges of the trash bag. There were layers of pictures. She pulled away the face of a brown woman and there was the dead body of a yellow man, pulled away the dead body of the yellow man and there was a battered face of a red woman, pulled away the battered face of a red woman and there was the empty and glazed eyes of a black starving child. There was no end.

She wasn't even halfway across the room, still only a yard or two away from the door frame because each picture was another picture.

Mama said from the floor, "You need some help, Rose?"

Rose shook her head. "No, I'm fine. You all keep doing what you're doing."

Violet's voiced was muffled from the closet. "I wonder how many magazines and books she had to destroy to get all this stuff."

Mama shrugged her shoulders. "Lilly always used to come home with bags full of magazines and books and all kinds of things. I think she got them by going through folks' trash."

Violet's muffled voice was amazed. "You mean she was a trash digger on top of everything else?" Her head came out the closet and her eyes were wide and almost innocent. "I'm sorry, really. I didn't mean that the way it sounded. You know I say things sometimes and . . . Sometimes things don't come out right and I'm still so angry with her, Mama."

Mama didn't say anything, just went to sorting clothes and Violet's head disappeared back in the closet and Rose wondered how they were all going to get through this. Get through being daughterless and sisterless and missing the child that they all loved best in spite of her fuck-ups for the rest of their days.

She said, "This was my favorite room in the house when we were little because we all used to come in here and sleep together at night. All sleep together and wake up and I thought that we would just keep right on doing that for the rest of our lives. Didn't you, Violet?"

Violet's muffled voice. "Oh, Rose. I thought that both of you would always be in touching and yelling distance. Nothing turned out the way I thought it would."

Rose went back to work, magazine paper crumpling in her hand easy into the trash bag. She was almost halfway across the room, wasn't even thinking anymore really about the faces she was tearing down and throwing away when she encountered herself. Herself staring back at her and surrounded by other brown and red and yellow and black faces.

Herself eighteen years old and big-bellied from Imani and eyes bleeding and glazed and she was so thin, looked like a picture of one of those starving brown and black and red and yellow women and she didn't remember ever being so frail or looking so absolutely sick. She hesitated, staring at herself and thinking how herself fit right in on the wall with all those other selves, that herself was cousin and sister and mother and daughter and lover of all those other selves.

Rose took a step back and scanned the room until she found a picture of Violet when she had long swinging hair and was still living with Jerome and still trying to make herself perfect, the burden of perfect making her skin dull and her eyes tired. She found a picture of Mama, Mama young and dressed in black and it was Daddy's funeral and Mama looked like at any second she would fall right into the grave with him. She found a picture of Imani sitting still on Mama's hardwood floors and staring quietly into the camera. She found a picture of Lilly, self-portrait, Lilly thin and yellow and bruised and eyes bleeding and face closed in on itself.

Herself and Imani and Violet and Lilly and Mama staring at her, indistinguishable from all the pictures of black and red and yellow and brown people on Lilly's wall unless she took a step back and really looked. And it made sense, but was still senseless and she took herself and Violet and Lilly and Mama and Imani down from the walls and threw them in the black trash bag. Black trash bag holding herself and Imani and Mama and Violet and Lilly. She didn't even think to call Mama and Violet and point it out and try to explain because there was nothing that she could say. All the time that she was trying to forget or rewrite her story, re-make herself Lilly keeping truth and keeping pictures and losing self trying to hold everyone else together.

Lilly's fragile yellow body nothing more than a map for everyone else's pain, just like Lilly was all the time saying, and no one really understood what she was talking about, and why it was impossible for her to be anything else but drug addict, prostitute, keeper of forgotten or distorted stories. Rose stared into the gaping black hole of the trash bag, stared at their pictures, and all the blood drained from her head until she was dizzy.

Studio Time

REARRANGING THE STUDIO, moving unfinished women to different corners and finished women to the
space just beneath the windows to get some sun and moving
the huge plastic garbage can where she kept odd pieces of
wood and stone real close to the door, right next to the
doorway because maybe with scraps right there in plain
sight and not hidden away there would be some kind of in-
spiration because her hands were just and simply numb.
Hands just and simply numb and hanging from her wrists
like ripe, rotten fruit hangs swollen from tree branches. She
was all the time waiting for her numb and ripe and rotten
hands to fall off and break open and dirty the stark and
clean hardwood floors of her studio.

Hands numb and ripe and rotten and mind constantly
busy. Still thinking about flower arrangements and casket
color and fried or baked chicken or maybe beef for later on
at the house. Still thinking about beer or wine or maybe
both and should she wear black or some other color because

Lilly didn't like to see anyone in a black anything but what did it matter when Lilly was gone? Still thinking like the funeral was ahead of her instead of behind and Lilly still waiting to be buried at the funeral home instead of buried in earth. Another way of holding on, of ignoring that Lilly was forever out of reach, gone. Just gone and her room cleaned out, her clothes and dolls thrown away or given to the Salvation Army, pictures torn from magazines ripped off the walls and buried in huge black plastic trash bags and the story that Lilly was trying to tell, even without words, never erased and gone like she was gone because it wasn't just Lilly's story and she was still trying to map the roads to her own truth like Lilly had mapped roads to everyone's pain.

She had dressed Imani for the funeral. Made sure that her little girl's dress was cleaned and ironed and her stockings matched her shoes and that her hair was done. All that primping and preening like Imani was going to a friend's party and there was going to be hot dogs and French fries and soda and cake and ice cream and clowns. There was nothing fun about putting on a pretty dress and getting hair done just so to go and bury your aunt. Nothing fun at all but Rose wanted Imani to have last good-byes and last memories other than waking up and being told that Aunt Lilly was all burnt up, ashes to ashes and dust to dust, but, please, try not to think about her that way. The things we tell children. Like there was any other way of thinking of a dead person besides dead.

The pain and shock of Lilly dead and Imani in her best dress and day of the funeral and back at the house and doorbell ringing, doorbell ringing and Imani opening the door

and Charles there. From all the way across the room, between them a mess of people and food and tables and chairs,
Rose watching Imani look into eyes like her eyes. The
longest moment of her life getting over to them, and both
of them quiet. She grabbed Imani like Charles was going to
pick her up and run with her. Squeezing on Imani's arm so
hard that she heard Imani's quick little intake of breath and
felt Imani's entire body go stiff beneath her fingers. Looking
at Charles and looking down into her child's face and she
let Imani loose and she was scared. She was scared and
angry and how, why did he have to show up here? She ran
trembling hands over Imani's hair. "Imani, go and see what
Grandma's doing, okay?" Imani going and turning every few
steps to look behind her and Rose waited until she was far
enough away so that she couldn't hear anything before she
turned on Charles. Charles standing there and looking almost just like she remembered him, a little older and a little
heavier. Seeing him standing there and seeing him hitting
her and yelling at her through walls and locked doors and
seeing herself leaving him when she was young and pregnant and scared and he was happy to let her go.

"What are you doing here?" She wasn't nice, too scared
and nervous to be nice and everything that went on before
between them and nothing she could do, no way she could
go back and make either of them different.

"I just wanted . . . I called almost a month ago and I
haven't heard anything from you. I just wanted . . ." He was
pale and confused and hesitating and she was surprised because he used words like other people used guns and knives.

Charles talking about wants and needs and her sister in

the ground. Charles always talking about what *he* was entitled to and what *he* deserved and she knew that he didn't deserve shit, not from her. "Lilly's dead, Charles. Her funeral's today."

"I didn't know. I wouldn't have come by if I had known."

"Didn't you see all the cars outside, the limo?"

"I just didn't think . . ."

Charles quiet and the year they spent together between them like something old and stale and Charles had put on weight, but his eyes were still the same. Imani's eyes. "That's right. You didn't think. Jesus, Charles. I can't believe you just showed up like this. What the hell are you thinking about?"

Charles looking past her, looking at Imani sitting on Mama's lap. "Is that her?"

Everything simple for Charles, always had been simple. "Is that her?" and Imani immediately his child. Her voice raising even though she was trying to keep quiet because of Lilly's funeral and Lilly not even settled in the ground. "Yes, that's her. But you're out of your mind if you think I'm going to let you get anywhere near her. You're fucking crazy."

"Okay. I know . . . I'm sorry. If I had known about Lilly, I wouldn't have come. I know you believe that. But I want to see her, Rose. I want to see her."

"I don't give a damn about what you want or need. Especially right now. I can't believe you."

People in the house staring and conversation slowing down and Taji making his way across the room to stand next to her. "You okay?"

"He just showed the fuck up, Taji. Charles just showed up like . . ."

244

"You want him here?"

"No. No, I don't want him here."

"You got to go," Taji said to Charles and Charles just stared at him, pale and eyes dull.

Charles wet his lips. "Look, I'm going to give you my number again. Talk to her about me, please. Please, Rose. If she doesn't want to see me, that's fine. But at least talk to her for me."

Charles' number crumpled in her fist.

Taji's hands on Charles' arm. "Man, this is not the time or place for this. You got to go." Taji pushing Charles out the door.

Charles shaking his head. "I didn't know about Lilly. I really didn't know. I've just been thinking lately about us like we were, thinking about everything that went wrong. Thinking about that child and thinking that she's maybe the one thing we did right."

Taji closed the door and she leaned into him, resting. Conversation slowly picked up again and Imani watched them from across the room.

Taji said, "You okay?"

She almost laughed, she was that close to tears. "No, I'm not okay."

Charles gone again but maybe back for good and Imani looking to her and waiting on answers about how come and why and what does it make me and who am I and Taji sleeping next to her at night and holding her carefully, and his "how come" all the time between them. When she was pregnant and living with Mama and hiding under tables and beds, in dark spaces of closets she figured out that there were no hiding places. Not until Lilly was dead and Taji was weary and Imani was waiting that she knew that there weren't any secrets worth keeping, that things left unsaid were never forgotten, like sharp knives digging beneath the skin.

Rose

IMANI SITTING ON THE WINDOWSILL in the living room, curled up with a thick blanket from her bed, forehead resting against glass and breath deep and easy. Rose watched her, tried to catalogue all the differences. Imani a few pounds heavier, body rounding and skin losing the first glow of childhood, her face becoming more itself and her eyes sad and laughter not as frequent and the little girl that Imani was gone forever and Rose sad and waiting, waiting for the woman. No easy thing, probably impossible thing, no falling into womanhood with smiles and laughter, just tears and wet staining the heart.

Rose went to her, put her hands on the coolness of her wild head, hair sticking up all over the place and Imani's scalp beneath the hair hot to the touch. "Hey. What you doing?"

Imani looking up at her and shrugging shoulders and smiling slightly. "Nothing. Just sitting here."

"Thinking?"

"No. Not thinking. Just sitting here."

"Can I sit with you?"

Imani curled into herself, making room on the windowsill. Cold air seeping beneath closed window and Imani offered her blanket. Rose hated cold against her skin at any time and they wrapped up in the blanket, windowsill small and cramped and no space between them. Imani's skin light brown and gleaming and her eyes light brown and sun around the edges and Rose stared at her and stared at her and tried to imagine Imani different, some other man's child, or Imani not living and breathing in the world at all. All the air left her body in a rush of panic and she reached out for Imani's warm flesh.

"I've been wanting to talk to you . . ." A bad place to begin, but there were no good beginnings and Imani wide-eyed and waiting and watching her and she had to get through it, had to get through it and say it because once it was said it was not something waiting out there to hurt them, not something leaving her child fragmented and in pieces, shaping past and history and family from imagination and wandering men never staying. "I've been wanting to talk to you for a while now, before Lilly died and then that happened and we had to get through it . . . And not to say that somebody you love dying like that is something that you ever get through . . . I think that we getting our breath back, though. And since we getting our breath back, I need to talk to you."

Imani just staring and black and brown and yellow and red and almost white women positioned all throughout the living room, black women standing four feet high or small and placed on the tops of tables or half done and leaning in corners, against furniture and doors. Her child grounded in blackness, black political consciousness and black dolls and black women all the time surrounding her.

"It's about your father, baby. You remember the man who came to Aunt Lilly's funeral? The one you opened the door for? I talked to him for a little while, but he didn't come inside."

"I remember." Imani patient and still, so still that Rose almost thought that she was uninterested, bored, but her eyes never leaving her face and her mouth open and loose and vulnerable, the pink of her tongue and the white of her teeth showing.

Rose said it all at once, because there was no easy way to say it and watched Imani's face go slack and watched Imani look down at herself real hard, touch herself like that quick something about her changed and was different and Rose felt her heart break because she was Mommy and this was not something that being Mommy could fix and not something that being Mommy could explain and being Mommy suddenly was not good enough and the first shock and separation and Imani still hers but always now someplace where she could not reach.

"You sure, Mommy?"

First thing out of her mouth. A logical question because all this time no names and no history and no face and no past and now all of those things and all of those things making her child something different than what she thought she was, than what she was always told that she was. "Yes, I'm sure."

249

There were no pictures because she had lost or thrown them all away. Pictures were not needed because Imani had seen him and she knew that Imani was thinking about Charles' eyes. Eyes so bright and so wide and so small and seeing things in this totally different way and it was the different way that had eventually been too much for them. His eyes unlike Taji's eyes or any of the eyes that she knew Imani had pieced together from the bits and pieces of the men that came in and out of her life. Men with no hair or hair locked down the back or huge or short Afros and beards and mustaches and shaven faces and glasses. Men man big and taking up all the space or compact and strong and knowing that all the space in the world didn't belong to them like Taji. No pictures of Charles in Imani's head because until now no reason for her to think that Charles was a possibility in her life, blood of her blood.

Rose told Imani all about her father and that time on South Street and how they were so different and still children and it wasn't anyone's fault, just the way that things happened sometimes. The way things happened sometimes and Imani had no father all of her life and now he wanted to see her because, well, that was the way things happened sometimes, too. Lilly being buried in a closed casket and no one seeing her face for the last good-bye or brushing fingers against her face for the last touch was also part of the mess of the way things happened and Rose really didn't think that her child could take any more things just happening to her.

Rose watching Imani try to take it all in, Imani stunned quiet to realize that whoever he was, whatever was in him, was also in her. In her the way that Rose and Lilly and Violet and Mama were in her. In her all the way to the bone, blood of her blood and flesh of her flesh. Imani looking down at her own skin, lighter than Rose's but not quite as light as Lilly's. Imani feeling her hair, hair thick like Rose's and Lilly's and Violet's and Mama's but not quite as thick and the curl was looser, softer. Imani's eyes a light, light brown that had the sun shining at its edges.

She and Lilly telling Imani all about the Civil Rights Movement so that she would never forget, and about Mama raising three daughters alone. Rose all the time creating black women and talking to them, Violet's heart weeping helplessly because Jerome was leaving her or they were leaving each other, pictures of brown and yellow and red and black people hanging on Lilly's wall, Lilly burnt and shriveled in the grave and forever gone. Imani all of those things and something else entirely that she hadn't even known about that was still a part of all of those things.

Imani quiet and still for so long that Rose asked, "You okay?"

"I'm fine. He wants to see me?"

"Yes, that's what he says."

"Do I have to?"

"Not if you don't want to. You don't have to do anything you don't want."

"Why you telling me, then?"

"I don't know. Because you been asking almost since you could speak and I . . . I don't know, I just wanted you to be mine. That's all. Just mine. And now that doesn't seem fair and that doesn't make any kind of sense. Something like that you needed to know and I just had to get over being scared and tell you."

Imani twisting the blanket in her hands, pulling the cover off of Rose, leaving Rose cold. "What were you scared of?"

Hard questions and no answers and she was fumbling through as best she could. "Oh, Imani . . . I was scared about how you would feel and how you would see yourself and how you would see me. I don't know, I was just scared."

Imani rushing into her lap, warm and almost too big to hold but she tried. Imani's arms tight around her and her face against her breasts and her hair beneath her chin, tickling her neck and no more laps, this the last time her little girl would fit comfortably in her arms without having to bend and twist and contort her body. She didn't say the rest, protecting her child because how could she say he looked like the people who brought us over here from Africa, how could she say he looked like the people who had us slaves for three hundred plus years, how could she say he looked like the people who strung us up and raped us all throughout the South and maimed and diminished us from sea to shining sea?

"It makes that much of a difference?" Imani's voice muffled against her lavender shirt.

Rose stroked her hair, and the exposed skin of her arms and legs. "I don't think so. You still my child. You think so? You in any way feel different?"

"I don't know. I don't think so, though." And then: "Mommy, were you ashamed?"

Rocking her child and rocking her child because this was important, this is what she had to get right to help Imani find an in to herself, a place inside to grow strong. "No, no, no. Never shamed. Never shamed of you or him or the decisions I made. How could I be when I got you out of all of it? When I got me out of all of it? Listen to me, now. He wasn't, he isn't a bad person, nothing about him is bad. Just the place and time and where we were at. We couldn't get past it and we couldn't get around it, nobody could really, and I was so hurt that I just went quiet inside. But I was never, never ashamed."

"Okay." And then: "I don't know if I want to see him."

"That's fine."

Imani resting against her, resting and her arms and hands tight around her and breathing easy.

Studio Time

HANDS ONCE AGAIN AND ALWAYS MOVING, moving over rough, dark wood and smooth, dull stone. Hands listening for the whisper, the hint, the shape of bone and blood, flesh and form. Hands moving slowly and rhythmically and with precision, with such confidence and sureness. No faltering here, hands refusing to be stunned still by grief or overwhelmed by memories of herself hanging devastated and dazed on Lilly's wall. No faltering and the weight that she was carrying for herself hanging on Lilly's wall completely lifted and she was light enough to be an artist, Imani's mommy.

Imani strong and laughing and going to be all right and the past wasn't crowding her vision, taking possession of her hands. Lilly dead and gone and the story she was trying to tell without words harsh and clear. Lilly knew, better than she and Mama and Violet and Taji and Charles, that they weren't living on the fringes of history, or changing history, they simply were.

She wanted Imani to know what Lilly knew instinctively without making herself ritual sacrifice—that all of it was written beneath the skin long before birth. Long before birth and what happened to them was sometimes cruel and ugly and sometimes not so bad at all but always just what happened.

Taji

S HEETS WARM FROM BOTH OF THEM against his skin, lights off and shadows playing along the walls and ceiling and floor. Taji watched as shadows got deeper and deeper and nighttime sky breaking and falling apart outside. Loving her and holding her and holding her child and thinking about other arms holding her, other hands touching her, other men inside of her, other men stuck forever at the corner and edges of her memory. Other men walking around with pieces of her that he had no right to claim, stories that he couldn't tell.

Rose out there a long time like everyone else, out there thrown, flung about and around revolution and murder, peace and love and no rest. No rest just people all the time guilt-stricken or horror-stricken, angry and loud, scared and quiet, entire communities shattered. Whole worlds changing and falling and nothing anyone could do but stand around and watch and maybe pick up the pieces if they weren't too sharp. Rose cutting herself on all those jagged edges, bleeding and clumsily fixing wounds and remaining silent and hoping for the best. Everyone hoping for the best because there was nothing else, nothing else to go back to and people all the time worrying and wondering how to go forward. People moving forward like Lilly and his sister up in New York, heroin and blood and oxygen pumping through the body. People moving forward shutting down schools and taking over or burning down entire city blocks. People moving forward like Rose with secrets and hidden other lives and hidden other selves and no words for any of it. People moving forward and getting nowhere, moving forward and staying in one place.

Shadows taking over the room because odd time between night and dawn and light fading and making cracks in the nighttime sky. Rose sleeping next to him, curled into her pillow and quilt, flesh and breath and hot. He moved closer to her, touching her and rolling into her and smelling her hair and skin and breath, curling into her warmth. Mornings like this and he didn't want to leave her, he wanted thousands of mornings with her next to him, trusting and open.

Stillness all around them, early dawn stillness and waking her in the stillness. And staying in the stillness, staying in the space between dreams and desire and longing and disappointment. Her skin brown and smooth and damp from sleep and the weight of the covers. Yellow cotton sheets of the bed cool and rumpled. Her hair in his face soft and thick and nappy. His hair down his back, beneath them. Her body long and slim and round and soft and beautiful and precious and not his. Thing that hurt him most lis-

257

tening to things unsaid in her kitchen, thing hardest to get over. Her body hers and not belonging to anyone before him and not belonging to anyone after him and he was hoping, all the time hoping, that he was it for her.

Sleep touching and sleep feeling and sleep moving. Touching her and before and after gone, just the absolute moment where they were at and into each other. Her body fluid and lyrical beneath and above and over him. Burning heat and explosion and exhausted quiet and the moment gone and the sky all kinds of different colors and before sneaking up on him.

Her face, her face and eyes watching him in the odd light and hair wild about her head and he just wanted her, wanted whatever she had to give, whatever she could give. Wanted her and trying to get over and get beyond before. Her eyes steady on him, sheet around her waist and breasts bare.

"Did you love him?" Tightness in his chest and throat because he didn't want to know and he needed to know. Loving her and needing to know her specifics, no generalization and no easy answers. His "How could you?" and "Why?" ignoring the intricacies and intimacies of her life. "How could you?" and "Why?" demanding parameters and boundaries and leaving her no room at all with him for self.

Her eyes watching him and small elegant hand reaching out for his face, fingers and palm resting and moving slightly against the stubble of his beard. Fingers causing hurt to spill beneath his balls and he tried to wipe it away because her eyes were wide and steady and there was no hurt intended.

"I loved him. And no, I can't regret that I was with him.

Imani makes that absolutely impossible. And no, I can't go back and wouldn't go back and do things differently. Because of him there is Imani and because of him there is me now. The only thing I should have done was claimed it all, not left it all secret and hovering and waiting to hurt. Believe me, baby, the absolute last thing I want to do is hurt you.

"I love you.

"But yes, I loved him, lived with him, slept with him, laughed with him. And when things didn't work out, when all that shit that went before us and had everything and nothing to do with us caught up with us, I was simply and thoroughly hurt."

Her words conjuring up pictures of things that he didn't want to know anything about and trying to get beneath her words, beyond his expectations and limitations, beyond his "How come?" and "Why?" What happened to her, happened to her, and he knew he had no right to question her motives, no right to pick her apart and make her past accountable to anyone black red brown yellow living in this land, make her carry the burden all by herself of three-hundred-plus years.

Long fingers of her elegant hand warm and callused against his skin, breath smelling of him and early morning and sleep lovemaking beating back at him. Her face like the faces of all those other brown red yellow black women flung from shore to shore, city to city, weeping and more weeping. Trying to find space where being red and black and brown and yellow was okay and not something to be fucked or fucked with, not something to be pitied and not something leaving red yellow brown black women wondering how or if they were ever going to get through it. Rose like all those women and he couldn't fault her for where she had looked, the stones she had overturned, history knocked from shelves and haphazardly arranged. He just wanted to know what she had found.

"Rose?" Everything that he wanted to ask stuck behind his teeth and beneath his tongue. He said again, "Rose?"

And her arms around him, holding him, her face against his neck. His arms around her. Rose, not some stranger woman, and who she was not easy and where she came from making her something else than what he thought she was, but no less loved. Rose not his and maybe staying with him because she loved him that hard.

She said, "I never said, Taji. I never said because I didn't know how to say it and be it and keep moving, you know? But who he was then and who I was then and what we had and didn't have together and who I am now all right. All of it all right and just what happened and I'm ready to keep moving now. Need to know that I can keep moving with you."

He thought about Imani, other man's child he loved, loved long before Rose. Maybe loved Rose because of Imani. Thought about Imani now all the time looking down at herself, looking inside herself. Thought about Rose and whole years of her life silenced and forgotten. Thought about Civil Rights and Black Power and Black Panthers and free love. Thought about us and them and them being inside of us, blood of our blood and flesh of our flesh long before Civil Rights and free love. No way to undo what's done, just living with it, and living with it living with and loving Rose and Imani. The night almost gone, almost gone and the sun dull in the sky.

Everything he needed in his arms. "Whoever you were, wherever you been, whatever you are now is who I love." His hands in her hair, fingers moving over her scalp. Not easy, none of it easy—starting with what you have, being who you are.

Sun dull in the sky and nighttime stars gently fading and breathing slowly down. They were nothing more than long limbs, arms and legs and chests, and beating hearts.

Shawne Johnson was born and raised in Philadelphia, Pennsylvania, where she now lives with her husband and two daughters. She received her undergraduate degree from Bennett College in Greensboro, North Carolina, and completed her master's degree in English literature at Temple University in Philadelphia. She was also a United States Peace Corps volunteer in Mozambique, Africa, and is currently working on her second novel.